All That Matters

Book two of the *Sweet Ever After* series

Elaine E. Sherwood

ALL THAT MATTERS
BOOK TWO OF THE SWEET EVER AFTER SERIES

*This is a work of fiction. All of the characters, names, incidents,
organizations, and dialogue in this novel are either the products
of the author's imagination or are used fictitiously.*

iUniverse books may be ordered through booksellers or by contacting:

*iUniverse LLC
1663 Liberty Drive
Bloomington, IN 47403
www.iuniverse.com
1-800-Authors (1-800-288-4677)*

*ISBN: 978-1-4917-4030-9 (sc)
ISBN: 978-1-4917-4031-6 (e)*

Library of Congress Control Number: 2014912381

Printed in the United States of America.

iUniverse rev. date: 8/25/2014

Dedication

This book is dedicated to the memory of my grandmother, Goldie Ethel Carpenter Rockwell. She always told me I was a smart girl and I could do anything I put my mind to...and she was right. I CAN. Love you, Grandma...always.

Acknowledgements

A dam Nugent (BluePineapple Design & Graphics). I love the cover picture. Thanks so much.

Nicole Colwell (Colwell Creative Content). Your help has been invaluable during the writing process of this book.

The Russian phrases are in the book as a result of help from Alex Breslov. Thanks Alex.

Thank you, Jack Tidlow, for continuing to be my dance partner. I know at times you need extreme patience!

Thank you, CyberDark Computing, for all your help. You literally saved this book from being lost in the black hole of cyberspace. You guys are the best!

And last, but not least, thank you, David Ripley (Studio 1262 Dance Academy), for your friendship, encouragement and patient instruction.

Chapter 1

Jimmy O'Brien, Vincenzo's band leader, had heard about Natalia and Vladimir Rusinko from a friend of a friend. He had been told that they had been Ballroom and Latin dance champions in Russia. They were in the United States to make an International name for themselves.

Finding dancers to round out the Vincenzo Dance Team had proven to be much harder than Jimmy had anticipated. He had contacted the Rusinkos and they had agreed to come for an audition. Final arrangements were made and a month later, he picked them up at the airport in Dixon.

He called Georgio from the airport to say they would be arriving at the ballroom in a couple of hours, barring any unforeseen difficulties.

Any professional dancing to represent the Vincenzo Restaurant and Ballroom had been put on hold until they had actually developed a dance "team." So far Ann, Bryce, Mama Rosa and Georgio were the whole team.

Everyone agreed to meet at the ballroom at ten o'clock on this blustery January morning. They were all very excited to meet this promising new couple.

Bobby looked like he had just crawled out of bed. His hair was sticking out in all directions, his eyes still puffy from sleep. His appearance this morning belied the fact that he was an extremely intelligent, highly motivated young man who was second in command under Bryce Peterson of Peterson Enterprise.

"Oh, come on man," Luke said dancing around his friend like Muhammad Ali, feigning a quick one-two punch to Bobby's ribs. "I worked all night and look at me. Fresh as a daisy."

Butch pushed his wet nose into Bobby's face.

"See, even Butch is still raring to go!"

Bobby groaned as he tried in vain to push the big, friendly dog away. His wife, Maria, watched this little interplay with a contented smile on her face. They had been "busy" until late last night. After all, they hadn't been married all that long and they were still "honeymooning."

Rosa and Georgio Vincenzo had always been early risers and they had been up for hours. Even though they had turned over ownership/operation of Vincenzo's Restaurant and Ballroom to Ann and Bryce Peterson, old habits were hard to break.

"The early bird, he get a worm, you know," Georgio said.

It was one of his favorite expressions. He would never understand why people so young wanted to stay in bed half the day. Mama Rosa just rolled her eyes and threw up her hands in exasperation.

"What you been doing all night anyway?" he continued with a wink at Mama.

Even after living in the United States for many years, his Italian accent was still noticeable, especially if he was excited...or angry. It was one of his most endearing qualities.

It had been a late night for John and Carla Benson too. John felt the weight of responsibility for all the financial matters involved in Peterson Enterprise and he needed his rest. That was his excuse anyway, for being grumpy this morning. No sleep.

Carla wasn't in any better shape. The dark circles under her eyes were proof of her sleepless night. She supervised the cleaning staff, plus the cooking and wait staff for Peterson Enterprise, as well as being the mother of a very active little boy.

Little JB hadn't felt like going to sleep until the wee hours of the morning. He had cried and fussed no matter what his parents tried. No amount of bouncing, singing, walking or book-reading helped.

His parents were in desperate need of coffee. John Bryce was now sleeping peacefully.

Bryce and Ann had taken a long, leisurely shower together; something they did routinely. They still arrived in plenty of time to help Mama Rosa get brunch on the table. Their home on the Peterson Estate was only a few minutes up the road from the ballroom, so the drive wasn't a long one.

The whole "family" was gathered and waiting with great expectations.

Chapter 2

Jimmy was at the airport as the plane landed. He recognized the Rusinkos immediately. They were hard to miss. The arrogant way they carried themselves triggered misgivings in Jimmy. Their condescending attitude when he stepped forward to meet them made the hair on the back of his neck stand up.

Right up front, Natalia let Jimmy know that they were doing him a huge favor by even coming for this interview. They were far too good to be associated with a small, backwater ballroom. Since they had not yet found a permanent position, they had agreed to come and dance.

They bickered back and forth in Russian from the back seat the whole way to Cedarville. The young man and woman who had carried their bags were apparently part of their entourage. So far, neither of them had said a word.

Well...we don't have to actually HIRE them, Jimmy thought, glancing at the couple in the rear view mirror. *I feel sorry for the young couple though, whoever they are!*

Georgio, being his usual outgoing self, welcomed them to his humble establishment with much theatrical fanfare. With great pride, he introduced them to the rest of the family.

"We are so happy to meet you. Come in, come in. Mama has fixed you a little something to eat."

The young couple hung back, obviously not knowing exactly what to do. The Rusinkos didn't bother to introduce them.

"And who are these two charming young people?" Georgio exclaimed enthusiastically, drawing them into the group.

"They are with us," Natalia said, barely giving them so much as a glance. "Victor and Anika Petrov."

Georgio took an immediate dislike to the Rusinkos, as did Butch, which was highly unusual for both of them.

Maybe it's the way they look us up and down that scares me, Ann thought as she stepped closer to Bryce. Bryce must have picked up the same vibe because his arm immediately went around her shoulders.

Bobby was instantly on the alert. He took a step forward, putting himself slightly in front of Maria. JB started crying so loudly that Carla and John excused themselves before heading for their apartment. Butch was standing beside Luke with the hair along his back standing up.

Luke put his hand on the big dog's head. He had learned to trust the dog's instincts. *I better pay close attention to these two,* he thought.

This was not the case with Victor and Anika, however. Butch trotted over to them, sat down and gave them his very best "smile." They were intimidated at first. After he whined and wiggled up to lean against Anika's leg they realized they had nothing to fear from their new, furry friend. Anika slowly reached down and ruffled the dog's ears, a shy smile on her face.

Natalia had a haughty way of looking down her long, skinny nose that made everyone feel somewhat uncomfortable. The bun that held her hair back tightly from her face gave her a sharp look that was accentuated by thin lips and a pointed chin. She was richly dressed in a long, fur coat and hat. Her leather, high-heeled boots came to her knees.

Without hesitation, she began laying down the rules. First, she demanded a room where she and her husband could rest. The food Mama had prepared was to be brought to them. When they had eaten and rested, they would proceed with the interview, including performing whatever dances were required. Natalia was definitely the one in charge.

"Pensa che ci sono contadini ignoranti," Georgio whispered to Mama. *She thinks we are ignorant peasants.* For once, Mama didn't argue.

Vladimir was sullen. On several occasions he was noted to take a healthy swig from a flask he tried to keep hidden in his very plush, heavy, winter coat. His once handsome face now had the look of someone who really enjoyed his Vodka.

Everyone noticed the way his bloodshot eyes kept returning to Ann's chest. The family stayed protectively close to her, especially Bryce and Luke.

No one was sure about Victor and Anika. What was their role in all of this? The situation became crystal clear when Natalia began barking orders at them in Russian, causing Anika to jerk to attention. Victor scurried toward their bags.

With his face beet red, Jimmy's next thought was, *Oh noooooo, this is worse than I expected! I feel awful for having brought these people here!*

Bryce came to his senses first.

"I'll show you to a room. Please follow me," he said politely.

He walked toward the hallway leading to the rooms kept available for visitors, leaving Ann under Georgio's watchful eye.

The "royal" couple swept past the rest of the group while Anika and Victor hurried after them, lugging the heavy suitcases. Even Bobby was speechless.

Grumbling all the way to the kitchen, Mama began preparing a tray of food, while Ann got the table service together. Butch now stayed close to Ann with every step she took, reinforcing that he sensed all was not well.

When the two obnoxious Russians were finally behind the closed door of their room, everyone breathed a sigh of relief. Anika and Victor stood in the hall, hand in hand, heads down.

Chapter 3

The men immediately gathered in the dining room to discuss this current embarrassing development.

Mama just shook her head in disgust as she motioned for Victor and Anika to follow her. She led the way into her cozy, warm kitchen. Pulling out two chairs, she indicated that they should sit. They sat down slowly, keeping their eyes fixed on Mama's face.

Still muttering to herself, she began bringing food out of the fridge. She spooned breakfast casserole into a pan. Maria put out plates and silverware. Ann poured big glasses of cold milk. The two bedraggled-looking young people watched, confusion written on their tired faces.

Their eyes grew wide as the delicious aromas of Mama's breakfast casserole and warm cinnamon buns wafted their way. They looked hesitantly at Mama as she set the food on the table in front of them.

Mama patted Anika's cheek.

"Go ahead. Mangiare, eat."

They didn't have any trouble understanding what she meant. They devoured the food so quickly it made Ann's heart ache to watch them.

After second helpings for both of them, Mama showed them to a room down the hall from the Rusinko's.

She opened the door and pushed them gently toward the big, soft bed.

"*Riposo.* You rest now."

Mama, Maria and Ann joined the men in the dining room. Mama was still sputtering in Italian as they sat down and poured coffee.

Luke was the first to speak.

"Dad, I think she's cut from the same cloth as Monica. We should steer clear. I don't care if they can dance!"

Monica had been Bryce's first wife. He knew all too well what Luke was talking about. He agreed with Luke, as did Rosa and Georgio, who had also been on the receiving end of Monica's vile behavior.

"Those poor kids. I wonder what their story is?" Bobby said. "They sure don't talk much."

"My guess is they don't speak any English," Ann commented as she sipped the hot cocoa Mama always made for her. "I know someone who speaks Russian. She's a young woman who works as a nurse practitioner at the hospital. I think I'll call her. Maybe she would be willing to help us."

As Ann and Bryce left to use the phone in the security office, they heard Jimmy apologizing to Georgio for bringing them.

"I swear. I didn't know they were so snooty and...rude," he finished lamely.

"That's okay, Jimmy, my boy," Georgio assured the contrite young man. "You had no way of knowing what they would be like. And besides, maybe we can help Victor and Anika!"

Chapter 4

Theresa O'Shay had worked at Cedarville Memorial Hospital for three years. She had just finished her shift when the switchboard paged her to tell her that Dr. Reynolds-Peterson was on the line for her. She knew Ann by reputation only. Since emergency medicine wasn't her area of expertise, Tess wondered why the doctor was asking for her.

When Ann explained the situation, Tess was only too willing to help out in any way that she could. Her parents had thought Russian was a silly language to study for someone who had lived in Vermont all her life. Where would she ever use it? But Tess was a headstrong young woman with a mind of her own. She believed nothing happened by chance. Besides, the language fascinated her.

Tess gathered her belongings. *I'll have to call Dad. He'll be shocked when I tell him I'll be using my Russian skills,* she thought with amusement. Ann had said she would send her son, Luke, to give her a ride. *I wonder what this Luke kid looks like,* she mused as she waited in the lobby by the front door.

Tess O'Shay was Irish with carrot-red hair and green eyes. She was tall for a girl at six feet and thin as a rail. It wasn't surprising that she didn't date much. Most of the men her age were just...too short. The boys in school had called her "scarecrow" or "toothpick."

Adding to her poor self image were the freckles that covered her skin. The front tooth that wasn't quite even with the rest of her teeth didn't help. She had learned early that words hurt. Even the girls had made fun of her. She sighed. *Luke Peterson probably won't be any different.*

A car with *Vincenzo's Restaurant and Ballroom* painted on the side pulled up into the circle in front of the hospital. *This must be him,* she thought. She sighed again, preparing herself to be gawked at. With downcast eyes, she subconsciously slouched a little, trying to make herself appear shorter.

She felt a light touch on her shoulder.

"Are you Theresa O'Shay?"

She took a deep breath and looked up...and up...into the most handsome face she had ever seen. She blushed to the roots of her hair.

"Yes," she finally managed to stammer. "You can call me, Tess."

As Luke gazed into her beautiful green eyes, his heart fluttered in a peculiar way. For several seconds, they just stared at each other.

"This way, Miss," Luke said quietly.

He guided a very flustered young lady into the front seat of the car.

Oh, my good God in heaven. I think I'm in love, was the first coherent thought that ran through her mind. She arranged her coat around her shaking knees to give her hands something to do.

The short ride to Vincenzo's was a silent one. Luke couldn't, for the life of him, think of anything to say. Tess just stared out the passenger side window, seemingly fascinated by the scenery they were passing.

Ann and Bryce met them at the front door. Ann watched Luke as he helped Tess with her coat. Bryce watched Tess blush as she thanked Luke. They gave each other a knowing look. This was certainly going to be an interesting afternoon!

Chapter 5

"Tess, I guess you already know my mom," Luke said as he began the introductions. "This is my dad, Bryce Peterson. This is Georgio Vincenzo and his beautiful wife, Rosa. We all call her Mama," he continued, smiling warmly at her. Next is Jimmy O'Brien, band leader for the ballroom. And last, but not least, this funny looking character is Bobby Rodriguez and his lovely wife, Maria."

"Don't listen to him," Bobby laughed. "He's just jealous of my manly good looks and fine physique."

Taking Tess by the hand, Mama led her to the table.

"Oh, for goodness sake," she groaned. "Pay no attention to those two. Can I get you something to eat or drink?"

"No, I'm good," Tess said deciding she was going to really enjoy being part of this happy-go-lucky family where everyone was trying to make her feel at home.

Bryce was just beginning to explain their situation in a little more detail when Natalia and Vladimir opened the door into the dining room.

Butch pulled himself up off the floor to watch the couple approach.

"Speak of the devil," Bobby mumbled, none too quietly.

Mama gave Bobby a stern look. He shrugged innocently.

Apparently, they were ready to dance. Natalia handed Georgio their music.

"Are you ready?" he asked before turning on the sound system.

"Of course, you stupid man. Why do you think we are standing here?" she replied with a sneer.

Jimmy cringed.

They were technically perfect, there was no doubt about that. They danced and smiled into each other's faces at the correct intervals. They made the appropriate loving gestures. They had good fluidity of movement. However, it took only minutes to recognize that the chemistry was definitely not there.

"I don't think they even like each other," Mama hissed in Georgio's ear.

Jimmy looked on in amazement. He had been told they were really top notch. If this performance had been stellar he might have been willing to overlook the rude behavior. After all, they had traveled a good distance to be here. They were probably tired. *Nobody is going to pay to watch these two dance and forget competition! We would never win,* he thought as he watched.

Georgio looked at Rosa with a raised eyebrow. Mama gave an almost imperceptible shake of her head. Neither of them were impressed.

Several different dances were performed. All of which were painful to watch. It was no wonder they were not attached to some other ballroom.

Georgio meandered over to the music table. He fiddled with some of the knobs on the pretense of adjusting the sound. Soon Bryce and Ann's music filled the ballroom. Then he winked at Mama. *Might as well show them what real dancing looks like.*

Unable to resist, Bryce took Ann in his arms, and swept her away in a beautiful waltz. Georgio and Rosa had taught them well. They had worked hard during their practice sessions, and the improvement in their technique was dramatic. It wasn't just the complicated footwork, or their graceful lines that made them spectacular to watch. It was their passion for each other that was mesmerizing.

"Now that's chemistry," Georgio stated, plenty loud enough for all to hear.

Everyone was entranced as they watched Ann and Bryce move as one across the floor. They seemed to be in a world of their own. Even Natalia didn't have anything to say as she watched from the sidelines. Vladimir's eyes were on Ann.

Hearing the music, Victor and Anika appeared in the doorway. As they watched, Anika's arms went around Victor, her head dropped to his shoulder.

"*Oni tak vmeste krasivi,*" she said quietly. *They are so beautiful together.*

Victor held her tight. "*Myi mozhem tak tantsevat',*" he replied wistfully. *We could dance like that.*

When the song ended, Bryce kissed Ann tenderly. Slowly they walked hand in hand back to the group. Turning on her heel, Natalia stalked out of the room. Vladimir followed.

Chapter 6

Seeing Victor and Anika, Bryce motioned them forward. "This is our friend, Tess," Bryce said. "Tess, this is Victor and Anika."

They were surprised when Tess spoke to them in fluent Russian. The rest of the afternoon was spent getting to know them.

Victor's mother, Helena, had been friends with Vladimir's parents in Russia. When Vladimir and his wife decided to come to America, Helena asked him to bring her son and daughter-in-law with them. She wanted the older man to be a mentor, of sorts, to her son while teaching him how to navigate the professional dance world.

In return, the two young people would work for them until their flight money was repaid. Helena was a proud woman. She had humbled herself in order to make these arrangements. She desperately wanted her son to have a better life. She knew America was the only place this was possible.

Victor and Anika were now working to pay off that debt, never having been told exactly how much they owed. Vladimir held their passports and green cards, so they were completely at his mercy.

They had traveled from city to city, interview to interview, without success. There was certainly no mentoring being done. They were nothing more than servants to Natalia and Vladimir.

Victor had come to believe that Vladimir never had any intention of letting them go.

Anika was tall when compared to Ann whose height was just under five feet. Her lank blonde hair was pulled back loosely in a ponytail. The wisps that had escaped the rubber band were floating around her thin face.

There were dark circles under her light blue eyes from lack of sleep. Her clothes were certainly not warm enough for a winter day in Vermont. Even though her English was limited she seemed to understand the intent of what was being said.

Victor was several inches taller than Anika, putting him at about six-foot-two. He too was very thin. Thick black hair fell over his forehead. Anger simmered in his dark eyes every time Natalia spoke harshly to Anika. Frustration over his inability to protect and provide for her burned deep in his gut.

They made a very handsome couple. Maybe that's what Natalia hated most about them. She and Vladimir had left youth behind years ago.

As time wore on without any success at finding a "home," the Rusinkos became more and more frustrated over their lack of gaining fame and fortune. They took it out on Anika and Victor. They had left for America full of pride, with the idea that people would be standing in line to hire them. That hadn't happened. They never considered the possibility that the fault was theirs.

Since it was approaching dinner time, Mama headed for the kitchen. Ann and Maria offered to help. In no time at all, everyone was enjoying a sumptuous pot roast. Conversation flowed back and forth effortlessly.

"Maybe we should see if our other guests want something to eat," Ann whispered to Bryce.

"I'll go ask them," Bryce volunteered.

Ann's eyes followed him as he walked away. Oh, how she loved him. He had saved her from a life of loneliness and despair. Since they had found each other, both of them finally felt whole.

When he came back, Ann could tell just by the way he walked that he wasn't happy. She also knew that being the gentleman he was, he wouldn't give voice to his feelings.

"They would like food brought to their room," was all he said.

Ann started to stand. Mama stopped her.

"I'll do it," she said as she marched toward the kitchen fairly spitting sparks as she went.

Chapter 7

After everyone had finished eating, the table was cleared. Much to Georgio's delight, Bobby suggested a game of cards. Jimmy offered to deal. Luke, Bobby and Georgio were loudly enthusiastic over their game. Accusations of cheating flew; mostly from Bobby. He always good-naturedly accused everyone else of hiding cards up their sleeves.

"No, it's not that we're cheating," Luke laughed. "You just can't play worth a darn."

Ann sat on Bryce's lap, thoroughly enjoying his hand caressing her arm as they chatted with Maria and Mama. They included Anika through Tess as much as possible. Tess was a delightful young woman with an easy manner that made Anika feel comfortable.

Anika confided to her that she and Victor were very apprehensive about what Natalia would do next. Anika was afraid of her. Tess wondered if the unpleasant woman had ever been physically abusive.

In her heart of hearts, Anika wished desperately that she and Victor could stay here with the Vincenzos. She liked them so much. Mama reminded her of Victor's mother. It made her terribly homesick.

She knew Victor was enjoying himself too. He was having a good time, even if he couldn't communicate effectively. He was teaching the other guys the Russian words for different things around the large room. They in turn told him the English words. Then they all laughed when he tried to imitate the pronunciation.

Victor was extremely interested in the card game. He picked up the rudiments of the game just by watching. He was invited to sit in on the next hand. Luke laughed uproariously when Victor won. Victor grinned as he scooped his toothpick winnings into a pile.

No one saw anything of the other guests the rest of the night. They were all thankful.

The evening ended around ten o'clock. It had been a long day and everyone was tired. Luke had to work the night shift at the police department starting at midnight. This gave him enough time to make sure Tess got home safely.

Mama had invited everyone back to the restaurant for breakfast the next morning. She promised pancakes; an all-time favorite. They were all dreading having to deal with Natalia and Vladimir, but it had to be done. Everyone agreed that they would keep looking for dancers. They were also worried about what would happen to Victor and Anika.

The ride home for Bryce and Ann was a quiet one, each lost in their own thoughts. Bryce knew Ann was upset over the events of the day. The harsh, cruel behavior was a reminder to her of what she herself had suffered as a teenager. He also knew she already loved Victor and Anika.

Bryce squeezed her hand. *She has a mother's heart, this little wife of mine,* he thought.

When they were finally in bed, snug under the covers, Ann voiced her concerns.

"Isn't there something we can do, Bryce?" she asked as she cuddled up close to his side, her head resting on his chest. "It breaks my heart to see how poorly they're dressed. And they're both so thin."

Hugging her close, Bryce kissed the top of her head.

"We'll see, sweetheart. We'll see. I think we can afford to rectify the financial situation for them. We'll need to keep Tess around for a while though, which I'm sure will make Luke happy. I wonder what they are qualified to do as far as job skills go? I don't think Victor will accept anything he thinks is charity. I'll talk to Bobby about it in the morning."

"Bryce, honey, you are a wonderful, generous man. Do you know that?" Ann said as she prepared to thank him in a way she knew they would both thoroughly enjoy.

Chapter 8

I t was about eight o'clock in the morning when everyone gathered around the table. The Rusinkos had not surfaced; neither had Victor and Anika. Ann was worried.

She looked at Bryce, concern in her eyes.

"Honey, do you think we should check on them?"

All of a sudden, Butch stood up. His body tensed as he looked in the direction of the guest rooms. The big dog was in motion just as screams erupted from down the hall.

All heads turned in the direction of the commotion. The door was open since Mama had been coming and going with food from the kitchen, so everyone witnessed what was happening.

Vladimir was violently shaking Anika. Her head snapped back against the wall. Then he slapped her hard across the face. Her screams continued as he ripped her shirt down the front. Pawing at her, he tried to kiss her, while forcing his knee between her legs. She was fighting like a little wildcat!

Butch lunged. His powerful jaws clamped down on Vladimir's ankle. In the next instant, Victor, shorter and thinner than Vladimir, plowed into the bigger man, grabbing him around the waist. He tried his best to get leverage enough to pull him off Anika.

Dropping Anika like a sack of potatoes, Vladimir kicked the dog in the head hard enough to dislodge his other foot. He hit Victor three times in quick succession; once in the eye, once in the mouth and once in the ribs. The young man slumped over gasping for breath.

A now enraged Vladimir began beating Victor without mercy. Butch was barking and darting in whenever there was an opening. Having never received any training as an attack dog, his instincts kicked in. Even with blood pouring from his mouth, he tried to intervene.

Anika continued to scream as she threw herself at this grown man, trying in vain to stop him from hurting her husband. Victor was curled up in a ball on the floor trying to protect his head from the vicious blows.

The dog barking, Anika screaming, Vladimir yelling curses... it was total chaos!

For a few seconds no one moved, stunned by what was happening. Released as one from their paralysis, they rushed to rescue Victor before Vladimir beat him to death.

Luke Peterson was six feet five inches tall and weighed two hundred and fifty pounds. Because of the time he spent in the gym, he had a body built of solid muscle.

Calling off the dog, he grabbed Vladimir by the scruff of his neck and threw him against the wall. The handcuffs he always carried were soon holding the drunken man's hands behind his back. Apparently, he had started drinking early!

Watching all this from the doorway of their room, Natalia began screaming, "That girl is a filthy slut. She has always wanted my husband."

She grabbed Anika's hair and tried to pull her to the floor. Bobby stepped in, pinning the out-of-control woman's arms behind her back.

"Call the police," a struggling Natalia demanded.

A shocked look quickly replaced her outrage when Luke pulled out his badge. He stuck it in her face.

"I AM the police. Now STEP BACK and SHUT UP."

Luke and Bobby took the offenders to the dining room. None too gently, they were pushed into two of the dining room chairs where they would stay until the situation could be brought under control.

"Butch, watch," Luke commanded.

Butch understood. He took up a position just out of reach of the Russian couple. A menacing growl rumbled deep in his thick chest. His eyes never wavered. Wisely, they didn't move.

This whole scenario seemed to have played out in a matter of just a few minutes. Ann was terrified. She clung to Bryce, fear etched on her pale face.

"Sweetheart, it's over. I won't let anything happen to you," Bryce said quietly against her hair as he embraced her. "Those kids are going to need you though. Are you okay to help them?"

"Yes...yes, I'm all right," Ann said, her voice still quivering. "Will you please get my medical bag from the car?"

Bryce gave her a quick hug.

"That's my girl."

Chapter 9

Victor had managed to drag himself to a sitting position with his back braced against the wall. Blood was running from a cut over his eye. His mouth was also bleeding from a split lip. Anika was close to hysteria as she crouched beside her husband. Hiding her face behind his shoulder, she sobbed.

Bryce helped Victor stand before heading to the car for Ann's bag. In the meantime, Ann tried her best to calm Anika. The poor girl was trembling from exertion and shock. With shaking fingers, she tried to pull her tattered blouse together.

"Let's get them into the kitchen so they can sit down," Georgio said as he took charge of the situation. "Mama, you better get some ice packs ready."

Luke came into the kitchen with a camera. He explained as best he could to Victor that he needed photographs to document the injuries they had sustained. They were both terrified. *Where is Tess? I need her!*

After the pictures were taken, Ann began an assessment of their injuries. It took eight stitches to close Victor's eyebrow, and another five closed the cut in his lip. Mama gave him an ice pack, which he gingerly held to his bruised face.

Ann knew he probably had a couple of broken ribs. She also knew from her experience working in the emergency room, that unless his lung was punctured, nothing could be done. There were no symptoms to indicate that that was the case, so in time, his ribs would heal.

Ann then turned her attention to Anika. The side of her face was badly bruised. Her eye was already swollen and slightly purple. There was a good sized goose-egg on the back of her head from being slammed against the wall. A bite mark was visible on her neck.

Fortunately, she was not seriously injured. She was, by far, more concerned about Victor than herself. Maria had gotten a blanket and wrapped it around the trembling girl's shoulders. Tears were streaming down Anika's cheeks.

Almost feeling the bruises herself, Ann could easily identify with the fear in Anika's eyes. *If it hadn't been for Dr. Mark and Oscar... NO! I won't allow myself to dwell on the past. The past is the past. I'm safe now,* she reminded herself.

In the dining room, Luke was reading Vladimir his rights. The charges would be assault, attempted rape, disorderly conduct and public intoxication for starters. At Luke's request, Bobby was documenting everything.

This was the scene Tess walked in on as she entered the ballroom. She hurried over to Luke, tossing her coat over a nearby chair.

"How can I help?"

He sighed with relief. He gave her a brief explanation of what had just happened. It was very important that Vladimir understood his rights so Tess read them again to him in Russian.

"Do you understand these rights as I have explained them?"

"*Da.*" Yes.

Do you have any questions?"

"*Net,*" he responded without looking up. *No.*

Natalia sat, silent as a corpse for a change. Nasty bullying tactics weren't going to get them out of trouble. It had always worked in the past, no matter the situation. Not this time. Vladimir had gone too far. This time there were witnesses. Natalia was seething inside.

When Vladimir was drunk, he didn't care who might be watching. He wanted what he wanted. This morning, he wanted Ann. She was too well protected by her husband, so he settled for Anika.

Victor wanted nothing to do with pressing charges or going to court. The very thought of it caused panic to well up inside him. After some discussion with Georgio, Bryce decided that no charges would be filed if the pair left the area and never came back. Victor and Anika were satisfied. They had no reason to trust the American legal system. They did, however, trust this family.

Natalia immediately began whining about the money they were owed for bringing those sniveling brats to this country.

When asked what the balance of the debt was, she hesitated for only a second before quickly shouting, "Five thousand American dollars."

Bryce suspected this was not quite accurate. Nevertheless, he wrote them a check for that amount.

Before handing it over, he stated, "I want passports, green cards, and any other items belonging to Anika and Victor. I want them now."

The look on his face served to sober Vladimir up pretty quickly. He readily agreed to all the stipulations that had been laid down. Retrieving the passports and green cards from his inside jacket pocket, he handed them over to Bryce.

"You will be leaving within the hour," Luke informed them.

He continued giving them his not-to-be-questioned instructions. "I'll be taking you to the bank to cash your check, then to the bus station where you will buy a ticket to anywhere you want to go, as long as it's away from the Cedarville-Dixon area. Now go pack your belongings."

Tess translated to make sure they clearly understood what was going to happen. She further explained that the pictures of Victor and Anika, verifying the injuries they had suffered, along with the written statements from everyone present, would be turned over to the police department if they returned. The result of causing any further problems for Victor and Anika would generate the same consequences.

They understood. It only took them thirty minutes to pack their suitcases.

Chapter 10

When Anika and Victor were told that Vladimir and Natalia were gone for good, a look of relief crossed their faces, followed quickly by one of utter despair.

Maria slid onto the bench beside Anika. She put her arm around the young woman's thin shoulders. They might not speak the same language, but Anika understood friendship when it was offered. She gave Maria a grateful little smile.

Ann sat down beside Victor and told him, through Tess, that it was a very brave thing he had done. He had saved his wife from being raped and beaten without any concern for his own safety.

He looked at Ann. *"Ya tyebya lyublyu!"* *I love her!* He then spoke softly to his distraught wife. *"Vsyo budet horosho."* *Everything will be okay.*

With tears still running down her cheeks, Anika moaned almost as though she was talking to herself.

"No monies. No home. What to do?"

Bryce and Ann exchanged a look.

Bryce smiled, and squatted down beside Anika where she was sitting next to Maria.

"Can you two dance?" he said almost jokingly. " We're still looking for dancers to help us make up a dance team."

Tess rapidly translated.

Both heads snapped up.

"*Da!*" *Yes!* Victor rattled off a sentence to Tess.

"They want to interview right now," Tess said.

Bryce tried to convince them that they were welcome to stay until they were recovered, then they could dance. The proud young man insisted. He wanted to do the responsible thing.

Everyone went into the ballroom. Anika asked for a fox trot. The pain was evident on Victor's face; nonetheless, he held himself erect and took his wife in his arms. After that, even with their injuries, they danced for their lives and it was breathtaking.

Bryce and Georgio hired them on the spot. Bryce explained that their pay would include the apartment across from Bobby and Maria. They would also get a salary plus dance clothes and benefits. Victor stared at him in disbelief.

"We hire? We home?" Anika managed to say, looking from face to face.

"Yes, you're hired, and yes, you have a home here for as long as you want to stay," Georgio exclaimed clapping his hands.

Vincenzo's Ballroom was back!

Chapter 11

Bryce assured them that they were exactly what Vincenzo's needed.

"It will be hard work, no doubt about that. Ann and I have never done anything like this before so your help will be invaluable. Georgio and Mama are the only ones with experience..."

"...but we are old," Georgio interjected. "We need fresh ideas and routines in order to compete. You and Anika, you bring us that."

"Спасибо," Victor said as he shook hands with Bryce and Georgio.

"Thank you." Tess translated.

Victor said something else in Russian to Tess. She smiled.

"He says they are American now and must speak English."

Tess saw no need at this time to explain the citizenship process. That could come later.

Several times, Victor practiced, "Thank you" by copying Tess and straining with the effort to get the pronunciation somewhat correct. His fat, painful lip didn't help.

He looked at Bryce, then at each person in the room.

"Thank you," he said, with such sincerity that every heart was touched.

Victor was at the end of his endurance. He and Anika were both ready to collapse from the exertion of dancing. The stress of the past several months with Vladimir and Natalie had also taken a toll. The day's events were the straws that broke the camel's back, so to speak. They could hardly hold their heads up.

Ann gave Victor a mild analgesic and told them to go get some rest. Off they went to their room. The rest of the family was just settling around the table in the kitchen when they heard another blood-curdling scream.

Alarm immediately made every heart jump as they again hurried to Victor and Anika's room. All over the floor were their clothes, ripped to shreds. Their suitcase lay open, the hinges broken.

Worst of all, Victor held the broken, twisted frame that had held the only picture he had of his parents as they danced together in their youth. The picture itself was torn in little pieces, and scattered across the bed.

"Damn! Oops, sorry, Mom," Luke said as he surveyed the damage. "I should have expected something like this and watched those two a little closer."

Apparently, they had sneaked into this room and ruined everything they could get their hands on. *What hateful, evil people.* Ann thought as she looked around sadly. *But what goes around, comes around, as they say.*

This was the final insult to this brave young man who had already endured so much. His face crumbled. Gasping sobs erupted from down deep. Victor pulled Anika close. They clung to each other and wept.

As Ann and Mama tried in vain to comfort the two broken-hearted young people, Bobby and Maria quietly gathered up the pieces of clothing and the suitcase. While everyone's attention was focused on Victor and Anika, they picked up all the tiny pieces of the picture that had been destroyed.

Ann finally got the kids into bed, in the same clothes they were wearing when they arrived, now the only ones they had. With the help of the medication, and from the stress of the day, they both fell asleep.

Bryce and Ann quietly left the room and closed the door. She looked up at Bryce, tears glistening on her eyelashes. He understood her so well. His arms went around her and he held her close. He didn't have to say anything. She knew everything would be all right.

Chapter 12

Bobby and Maria said they had some errands to run and they would be back in time for dinner.

Bobby kissed Mama's plump cheek.

"Never fear, Mama, we'll be back in time to eat."

Mama laughed as she swatted Bobby's arm.

"Go on then, you two. *Andare*, GO!"

Tess said she would be back as soon as she could find someone to cover her shift at the hospital. She headed for the door, then stopped and ran back to Mama, giving her a hug.

"See you later," she called as she turned and ran out the door.

"Everyone...they know where to come when it's time to eat," Mama chuckled.

She hadn't been this happy since before her daughter passed away. She tried to hide it, but she loved having so many people around. They were all her "children and grandchildren." In her mind, it wasn't necessarily blood ties that made a family. It was love.

The couch in front of the fireplace looked very inviting to Ann and Bryce, so they decided to build a fire and curl up together for the remainder of the afternoon. They had made many happy memories on this very couch and Bryce was hoping to relive some of them. The look Ann gave him told him she was remembering too.

Georgio and Mama went to their apartment to get some rest. It had been a hard couple of days for everyone.

Luke and Butch headed out so the big dog could get a much needed run and Luke needed some air...and some time to think. *Tess, wow. I really like her. I hope Victor is a slow learner,* he mused. *That way we'll need her coming around for a good long time.*

It wasn't long before Anika reappeared. She walked over and stood in front of the fire.

"Are you okay, Anika?" Ann said, concern in her voice and on her face.

"Hurt," she replied, cupping her bruised cheek with her hand.

The bruise on her cheek was now a dark purple and Ann knew it must be sore by the way the exhausted-looking young woman moved her mouth when she tried to talk.

"I worry," she continued hesitantly, trying to find the right words in English.

Tears welled up in her eyes.

Ann moved over, making room between herself and Bryce. She patted the seat and Anika dropped down onto the couch. Ann pulled her close, pushing her hair back from her face.

Anika had missed a mother's touch all her life. It felt so good to snuggle into the curve of Ann's arm. Bryce met Ann's eyes over the top of a tousled blonde head. *Ahhhh, we have another daughter,* he thought contentedly to himself as he reached over and rubbed the back of Ann's neck. The warmth of human closeness worked its magic and Anika was soon asleep, her head on Ann's shoulder.

I guess my plans will have to wait until later, Bryce thought as he stroked Ann's hair. He smiled into her beautiful blue eyes and thought, *there will always be another time.*

Chapter 13

Rosa Vincenzo smiled to herself as she bustled around the kitchen getting dinner ready. Georgio was putting tossed salad together and singing a little song in Italian.

Mama had been so worried about him in the period following their daughter's death. If Ann and Bryce had not come when they did...she was afraid to think of what might have happened.

Now the house was full of laughter, the restaurant had reopened and business was booming. *And now, dancing again. I would have never believed it was possible,* Mama thought. She popped the lasagna into the oven, knowing it would be delicious.

Apparently, Luke had caught up with Tess somewhere along the way because they arrived together. She was giggling. Luke had a contrite little smile on his face. Butch followed behind, sworn to secrecy, it seemed.

The smell of lasagna was just beginning to waft through the kitchen door when Bobby and Maria appeared, carrying all kinds of bags and boxes. Each was dragging a large suitcase. They had excited silly grins on their faces.

Hearing all the commotion, Anika woke up with a start. As she slept she had slid in Bryce's direction and was leaning on his chest. He didn't seem to mind. He gave her a hug before sending her off to wake up Victor.

"Hurry up you guys, come on. What ya gonna do, sleep all day?" Bobby yelled as soon as he saw Victor and Anika. "We have surprises for you!"

Bobby explained and Tess translated.

"We bought Christmas presents for you," Bobby said. "Since you missed Christmas with us, presents are in order. Come on Victor... Anika. This stuff is for you!"

As they opened their "presents" each found a warm winter jacket, hats, gloves, scarves, jeans, sweaters, shirts, underwear, PJ's and socks. Victor got a leather wallet and a shaving kit. Anika got a cute little purse and inside was lipstick, mascara, a comb and a brush.

"Oh Bryce," Ann breathed against his cheek. She kissed him gently. "Bless their hearts!"

Maria had measured the ruined clothes to approximate the sizes, then she and Bobby had gone shopping. They didn't have anything to go by for shoe sizes so those would have to be purchased later.

Victor and Anika's shocked looks turned to wonder and then embarrassment.

Realizing they were uncomfortable with all this attention, Bobby slapped Victor on the knee and shouted, "Merry Christmas to all, and to all a good night!"

"You, Bobby Rodriguez, are a bonehead," Luke joked.

With that said, he cuffed his friend on the back of the head.

"Hey, you big lug, who do you think you are anyway?"

Fake punches were thrown until Luke, being the taller of the two by far, picked Bobby up as if he were weightless. Bobby, not to be outdone, wrapped his arms around Luke's neck and gave him a big sloppy kiss on the cheek.

In his best "girl voice" he said, "You're *so* big and strong," appropriately batting his eyelashes.

Not understanding what was going on, Anika initially was frightened by this rowdy behavior and was holding on to Victor's arm. But as soon as everyone started laughing at these antics, she realized it was all in fun. Anika started to giggle. Victor tried very hard NOT to laugh and hurt his battered face.

The "happy couple" finally sat down and Bobby said, "Oh, one more thing."

He pulled a picture frame from a box.

He and Maria had painstakingly glued all the pieces of Victor's picture back together; that's what had taken them so long. Then they put it in a beautiful ceramic frame.

Victor stared at the picture and then looked at Bobby. He struggled to control the emotions that were bubbling just below the surface.

"I don't know what to say," he said through Tess.

"I know a photographer that specializes in restoring old photos. Later in the week we can go into Dixon and take your picture to him. I think it will be as good as new," Bobby continued excitedly.

"I am in your debt," Victor said, wiping his eyes with the back of his hand.

A big smile spread across Bobby's face.

"There is no debt between friends," he said with sincerity.

Tess translated.

In that moment, a friendship was forged that would last a lifetime. Ann was so proud of Bobby and Maria. They had done a very kind and thoughtful thing. No one could have more effectively made Victor and Anika feel that they were finally "home."

As everyone sat down to eat, the two new additions to the family began to talk openly about their lives in Russia.

Chapter 14

Anika had been raised in an orphanage, having been left there as an infant by a young woman without the means to care for her. She had always loved to dance and at sixteen, when she could no longer live at the orphanage, she got a job cleaning at a dance studio in Moscow. As she pushed her mop across the highly polished wooden floors, she would imagine herself floating gracefully around the ballroom in the arms of a handsome prince.

Over a bakery near the studio, she found a tiny flat just big enough for a rickety bed, a wash stand and some crates where she stowed her few possessions. In the wee hours of the morning, and in exchange for her rent, she helped to make the bread and fine pastries offered for sale when the shop opened later in the day.

The owner of the shop was a widower with several unruly children. He gave her all the food she could eat if she kept an eye on his three little boys and two girls so he could have some peace and quiet in the late afternoons after the shop closed.

He made it clear to Anika that, even though he was several years her senior, he appreciated her comely appearance and good work ethic. He would readily marry her in order to provide a mother for his children.

She would never want for anything and it would be a strictly business arrangement with no strings attached. He was a nice man and Anika was flattered, but he wasn't the handsome prince she danced with every night in her dreams.

Her life was busy, albeit lonely, with baking in the early mornings, watching the children after they came home from school in the afternoons and cleaning the dance studio in the evenings.

However, she stubbornly refused to feel sorry for herself. She had it much better than some of the women and children she saw on the streets...begging. When she fell into bed every night, exhausted, she was just thankful to have made it through another day. And she could always marry the fat little baker...

Chapter 15

Victor's parents had been Russian dance champions in their day. Victor Sr. had died unexpectedly at the height of their career leaving a young wife and son. Helena Petrov had to find a way to support herself and her son, so she got a job teaching dance. Young Victor often came with his mother and watched.

As he got older, his mother began teaching him. Soon he was a favorite "spare partner" at the studio. If a young lady didn't have a partner for the lesson, Victor gallantly stepped in. Helena sometimes suspected the girls intentionally came without partners just to dance with her handsome, charming son!

This just happened to be the studio that Anika cleaned. One afternoon, she arrived just as Victor Jr. and Helena were leaving. As time went on, Anika came to work early every day, hoping Victor would still be there. He looked remarkably like the man in her dreams; a thought that made her feel hot all over and slightly embarrassed for reasons she couldn't explain.

Anika had a delicate beauty that drew Victor in like a moth to a flame. In his eyes, none of the other girls could hold a candle to her. They began watching the last class of the day together and getting to know each other.

In no time at all, they became dance partners. Helena had begun teaching them after the regular students left for the day. Victor would stay to help Anika do the cleaning so that she would not get behind and lose her job. Their technique was exceptionally good and as they fell in love, their chemistry was something they didn't have to learn.

They were married in the little stone church that Helena attended. *So young,* she thought as she watched them together. *Only eighteen. They are so much like his father and me. I pray they will be happy together for the rest of their lives.* She had known from the beginning that they were meant to be together, so she gave them her blessing.

Chapter 16

Helena barely made enough money to pay rent and buy groceries. She certainly didn't have enough to launch a professional career for her son and daughter-in-law.

She also knew exceptional dancing when she saw it. She had confidence that, with time and experience, they would be good enough to make their way to the top of the dance world.

She eventually came up with the plan, which involved Vladimir Rusinko who she knew was leaving with his wife to come to America. The arrangements were made and Victor and Anika left Russia with their hearts full of hope. Helena would miss them desperately, but she wanted more for her son than being a dance instructor in a second rate studio making a pitiful amount of money.

"And the rest is history," Victor finished as Tess kept up with the conversation. "I miss Mama. I haven't heard from her in months. We never stayed in one place long enough to receive mail. I am worried about her."

"Well, gee whiz, man, write a letter. We can mail it tomorrow," Bobby said. "You've got a permanent address now!"

With this declaration, Bobby decided they should celebrate with his famous milkshakes, so off the four of them went to the kitchen. Tess and Luke trailed along behind, claiming they felt the need for ice cream too. Besides, Tess might be required to translate something.

"Hey, if you make a big mess in Mama's kitchen, you will be in big trouble," Georgio called after them.

He sounded angry. Victor and Anika stopped short and looked back. The grin on his face proved his bark was worse than his bite, something for which he was well known to the rest of the family.

Georgio turned to Bryce and Ann.

"You did a fine job handling everything that happened yesterday and today. My ballroom is in good hands," he said.

Having no living relatives, he and Rosa had turned the restaurant over to Bryce and Ann with the agreement that they would have a life time living arrangement in their own apartment.

He hugged Ann and pinched her cheeks as if she was a small child.

He and Mama headed off to their apartment. Bryce went out to warm up the car as Ann headed for the kitchen, where she gave Victor more pain medication. She noticed Luke was sitting next to Tess, not paying much attention to his milkshake.

Bryce appeared with Ann's coat.

"Bobby, when you kids are done here, why don't you and Maria show Victor and Anika their apartment? Luke, maybe you could see that Tess gets home okay. Get some sleep everyone. Tomorrow will be a busy day."

Good nights were said, and hugs exchanged all around. This was also new to Victor and Anika, but they had no problem joining in.

Ann sighed with contentment as they pulled away from the ballroom and headed up the road. They were anxious to get home. The last two days had been stressful, especially for Ann. Memories long buried had come rushing to the surface, leaving her shaken. They needed peace and quiet as well as the comfort of each other's arms.

Ok, I've waited just about long enough, Bryce thought as he squeezed Ann's hand, which happened to be resting on his thigh.

Chapter 17

As the weeks passed, bruises faded, cuts healed, souls and minds were mended. Victor and Anika were becoming more confident as they picked up new English words every day. Both had gained weight, thanks to Mama's cooking. They looked healthy and happy, with their individual personalities beginning to become evident.

Victor could hold his own with Bobby and Luke, having discovered a surprisingly dry sense of humor. His dark good looks contrasted beautifully to Anika's fair, delicate beauty.

As her blonde hair grew thick and long, Anika had developed all the curves that would look great in an evening gown. She tended to be a bit "ditzy" jumping up and down when she was excited; and she was almost always excited about something these days. It was as though the whole world had suddenly opened up to her.

She loved Ann and Bryce dearly, often calling Bryce *Papa*, which never failed to put a tender smile on his face. Ann had become the mother she never knew. Anika exuded happiness. It was a joy just to be around her.

Victor was anxious to get to work. He and Anika were soon going through the music that had been standards for the Vincenzos when they were European champions.

Victor told Bobby, "You make good dance if work hard."

"Are you kidding, man? Good dance is built into my Hispanic genetic material. I don't have to work at it, amigo."

"Ha!" Victor laughed. "You dance with two left foot."

Bobby cracked up. He did his version of a Cha Cha Cha, something Victor found hilarious.

Chapter 18

I t was beginning to look like the dance team was up to four couples as Victor and Anika began teaching Bobby and Maria the basics of professional dancing.

No one escaped the rigorous schedule that Victor established for making Vincenzo's a top dance team; not even Georgio and Rosa. Victor was an ambitious perfectionist. He definitely knew what he was doing when it came to dancing. His mother had taught him well.

He and Anika were stunning together. They were the total package. They had beautiful lines, grace, musicality, technique and, of course, chemistry. Georgio and Mama knew excellent dancing when they saw it. They were excited about the chance the team now had in the competitive arena.

Bryce and Ann had a special "something" that could not be taught. With Georgio and Rosa's encouragement and guidance, their technique was now very good.

Bryce had taken some lessons years ago before he met Ann so he wasn't totally lost. It was altogether different for Ann. She had never danced before she met Bryce. She did possess natural talent and she could follow Bryce without any difficulty at all. They were magical when they danced together.

The Latin dances were definitely Bobby and Maria's forte. Victor kept harping away at their footwork and posture until they slowly improved. There was no mistaking their passion for the dance and for each other.

Bringing up the anchor leg of the team were tried and true professionals, European Ballroom and Latin champions, Georgio and Rosa Vincenzo. In their sixties, they were probably one of the oldest couples on the Dixon dance circuit.

However, no one counted them out because of their age. They were still a pair to watch. They had maturity and experience on their side and they had an elegance about them that couldn't be denied.

It had been agreed upon right from the start that Anika and Victor would assume the role as Vincenzo's dance team leaders and choreographers.

When they objected, Georgio explained that he and Mama were just too old to take on the responsibility. Competition would require fresh ideas, new innovative dance patterns and boundless energy.

"We will be happy to provide support and the benefit of our experience. We will even dance," he chuckled. "But you are young and vibrant. You two kids are exactly what we need to make the team a success. You go, do what your Mama taught you! We are all very proud of you."

"I humble and thank you," was Victor's sincere response as he hugged the older man.

Chapter 19

Everyone had worked hard and it was time to get dressed up for a trip to Dixon for dining and dancing at Andre's. Claire Lafontaine, Ann's long time friend and seamstress, had fashioned new evening clothes for everyone.

Bobby couldn't help swaggering around as he complimented himself on what a fine looking man he was. Luke and Victor soon put him in his place, making sure he understood it was the clothes, not the man.

Everyone piled into the limo that had been rented for the occasion. It was an hour drive to Dixon and everyone was enjoying the ride.

Bryce pulled Ann close.

"You are the loveliest woman who was ever born," he whispered in her ear.

"And you are, by far, the handsomest man, my love," was Ann's heartfelt response.

She smiled up into his warm, hazel eyes, seeing once again the incredible love he had for her.

They never had trouble being "alone" together no matter how many people happened to be around. It was almost as though one could not breathe without the other.

Georgio had called ahead to ask if Andre would have an open table. Andre was the bachelor, Frenchman, owner/operator of *Andres,* a posh restaurant/ballroom in Dixon.

"But of course," was his immediate reply.

"He will move heaven and earth to make sure a table is open for you, Ann," Bryce teased. "He has a crush on you, you know and why wouldn't he?"

Ann just shook her head. She had to admit to herself, it seemed to be true. Andre had been smitten with her from the moment Bryce had introduced her.

"You silly man. I think it's only because I can speak French," she replied with contrived seriousness.

Victor and Anika were so excited! They had never been to such an elite restaurant. Bobby and Maria were almost as bad. They couldn't wait to introduce their new friends to the world of fine dining and dancing.

Vincenzo's had been open on the usual nights, but Victor and Anika had preferred to stay in their apartment. They didn't feel quite ready to face a crowd. Although they had worked hard on their language skills, they were still a little self-conscious about their English. They just weren't sure how they would be accepted. This would be their introduction into Dixon society.

Jimmy had told Georgio he would meet everyone at the restaurant. Getting there early was part of his plan. He purposely took a seat at the bar with a good view of the entryway so that he could observe, unnoticed. Having not seen Victor and Anika since the Rusinko fiasco, he wondered what they looked like "cleaned up."

He was certainly not disappointed. The influence of the "Peterson Clan" had worked wonders. They were a stunning couple. Although appearing somewhat stoic and serious, or maybe that was just a Russian thing, they moved with grace and confidence.

When they were introduced to Andre as the team leaders, they accepted his handshake with maturity beyond their years. Bryce and Ann were very proud of them both.

Everyone was surprised when Luke showed up with Tess on his arm. They made a handsome couple and the big smile on Luke's face spoke volumes.

Chapter 20

D inner was delicious. Andre, as predicted, fluttered around Ann like a nervous little hummingbird. Ann didn't dare look at Bryce. She knew she would see a smirk on his face and it would make her laugh. She would never do anything to hurt Andre's feelings, but sometimes he could be a little much.

When the dancing began with a waltz, Bryce and Ann were the first couple to take the floor.

Georgio and Rosa followed.

"Let us old folks show you kids how it's done," Georgio said, his hand under Mama's elbow.

Other couples were hesitant to join the dancing, preferring to sit and watch the artistry that Bryce and Ann created. If partnered with any other person, neither of them would have been above average as dancers. Together, they were breathtakingly beautiful.

The waltz was also a favorite of Georgio and Rosa's. They had danced competitively for many years in Italy, eventually in other countries, becoming European Champions.

They may have slowed down a bit, but the expertise, the gracefulness, the poise, how best to present themselves...all the things that experience teaches, were still there. Even with their silver hair and their somewhat portly figures, they still had the "it" factor.

Jimmy could not have been more pleased. The Vincenzo team might be newcomers to the dance world, but they were as good as, or better than, any other team he had seen; and he had made it his business to check out other teams. The reaction of the other guests who were watching was just as Jimmy had expected. They were fascinated by what they saw.

The second song had an upbeat Latin rhythm. Bobby was instantly on his feet.

"Now it's our turn," he laughed as he spun Maria in a wild circle. He began to dance with abandon without any regard for what Victor and Anika had patiently taught him.

Victor slapped his forehead and then buried his face in his hands.

"Oh, God! Help," he breathed.

Almost before his prayer had left his lips Maria grabbed his hand, tugging him toward the dance floor. Bobby did the same with Anika. Soon the four of them were dancing up a storm and having fun.

Jimmy was impressed. Bobby and Maria were definitely rough around the edges, but the potential was there. Victor and Anika, on the other hand, were excellent. All they needed was experience. During one of the breaks, he asked if they would be ready to compete by the end of the month. Everyone stared; mouths open.

"You have to get your feet wet sometime and I think you're ready," Jimmy said with confidence. "There's a small, more informal, pre-season competition at one of the other local ballrooms. I think it would be a good place for you guys to start.

"Get feet wet? What mean?" Victor said, frown lines appearing on his brow. "Bobby is, how you say...cannon loose, but feet dry. He bring down team score."

Everyone laughed including Bobby.

"I think you mean loose cannon, Amigo. But I'll do my best to reign in my enthusiasm when we compete. After all, I want us to win!"

They all agreed they would like to try.

"It sometimes takes many years to be recognized in the dance world. Don't expect to win the first time out of the gate," Georgio warned sternly. "I don't want you all to get your hopes up too high."

"What mean 'out of gate'?" Victor asked with a puzzled look on his face. "English! Very confuse."

Chapter 21

They did not win as a team, but this did not dampen their spirits. They had gotten a taste of competition and they were excited about the prospect of trying it again. Georgio and Rosa did win first place in the Fox Trot.

"Guess we haven't lost our edge," Georgio whispered to Mama.

They were somewhat embarrassed by the loud whistling and hooting from Bobby when they accepted the blue ribbon. Luke and Victor just exchanged knowing looks as if he were their unruly child.

"No one can fault his loyalty," Luke commented with a chuckle.

Jimmy had been right. This competition was small, only four teams had participated, but the experience proved invaluable. Now they had a better idea of how things were done and what was expected of them as a team, as well as individual couples. Bobby was somewhat sobered by the experience; a rare occurrence.

"Wow, Victor. You were right! I'm going to have to step up my game," Bobby commented on the way home. "But no problem. We're up for it aren't we, Baby?" he said as he kissed Maria. "I have to say we were the best looking team out there though."

Victor just shook his head.

One important lesson they learned was that they would definitely need someone to take over the responsibilities of wardrobe, hair and makeup; all those sorts of little things that Gloria Hamilton had done for them. When she passed away, no one else had the time or the skills to take her place.

They would need to dress professionally, as well as act professionally, a point driven home to Bobby by Victor. They needed to establish their own unique "look" and they couldn't do that without help.

Chapter 22

A t the beauty shop in Cedarville where Ann got her hair trimmed, there was a young Asian girl who often took care of her. Asia Kim was a very quiet, shy, young woman, probably in her early 20's.

The other girls in the shop frequently whispered about her when they thought she couldn't hear; then again, maybe they didn't care if she heard. It was apparent to Ann that Asia didn't "fit in" with the other girls who worked there.

Nothing ever showed on her face to indicate that their conversations about her bothered her. She simply went about her work. Ann couldn't believe the comments didn't hurt.

She was petite and her long, straight, black hair fell to her waist. Her black eyes were just slits in her round, flat face. She wasn't a pretty girl, but there was something hauntingly appealing about her.

Maybe it was the graceful movements of her hands as she worked to make every woman beautiful, or maybe it was her polite, quiet manner. Whatever it was, Ann felt drawn to her and always waited for her chair to be empty.

No matter how hard she tried, Ann could never draw Asia into a conversation. Her English was extremely limited and she struggled to answer basic questions.

One Tuesday morning Bryce drove Ann in to Cedarville to get her hair done. He dropped her off at the door with assurance that he would be back to pick her up in about an hour. When she entered the shop, there were two other girls besides Asia working. Each of them had a customer. Ann took a seat to wait her turn.

The other girls, as well as one of the customers, were giggling and glancing at Asia. Ann couldn't see anything funny. Their behavior made her more than a little disgusted.

As Asia finished with her customer, she made her way between the chairs carrying several combs and a blow dryer. The girl working at the next chair stuck her foot out just enough for Asia to catch her toe. She fell headlong. The combs went flying every which way as the blow dryer skittered across the floor ending up at Ann's feet.

Laughter erupted.

Asia quickly got up and began scurrying around gathering up the combs; head down, her hair falling forward to cover her face. Ann picked up the blow dryer. As she handed it to Asia, their eyes met only for a second. Ann saw tears...and blood.

Before Ann could say or do anything, Asia had thrown everything she had picked up into her work station chair and headed for the door. The laughter got louder. Asia put her hands over her ears and ran.

Ann was out the door right behind her.

Chapter 23

A nn followed the embarrassed young woman out onto the sidewalk.

"Asia, wait. Please wait," Ann called after her.

Her pace didn't slow. Ann had to run to catch up with her. Asia finally stopped when Ann grabbed her elbow. She slowly turned around without looking up. Tears mixed with blood ran unchecked down her face. Her mouth and nose were bleeding.

Taking some tissues from her pocket, Ann dabbed the blood from her nose and lip. The physical injuries didn't look serious. Nonetheless, Asia was obviously extremely upset.

Bryce was across the street at the hardware store talking to the owner, Clem Burns. As soon as he saw Ann run out of the shop, he immediately excused himself and hurried toward her.

"Honey, what happened?" he asked, his voice full of concern.

He put one arm around Ann, the other around the trembling girl. Asia collapsed against Ann's shoulder as the sobs shook her tiny frame.

"Let's get her home. I'll need to clean her up before I can tell if she needs further medical attention," Ann said as she and Bryce propped the young woman up.

Asia tried to walk, but stress that had accumulated over several years finally boiled over. She would have collapsed if Bryce had not caught her. He picked her up and with long, quick strides, headed for their car.

He gently sat Asia down in the front seat; Ann slid in beside her. The poor girl's strength seemed to be completely depleted. All she could manage was to lean against Ann for support.

As Bryce drove toward home Ann explained what had happened. He snorted in disgust. Ann knew he would be making a call to the owner of the beauty shop. She couldn't help smiling to herself. She could see owning a beauty shop in their future.

"She can stay in the spare room until we get things sorted out," he said as he glanced at Ann. "Do you think she's badly injured? Maybe we should take her to the emergency room for an x-ray or something."

"No, I think she will be better off with us. The bleeding has already stopped. I think she just hit her nose when she fell. I don't see a cut on the outside of her mouth, one of her teeth might have cut the inside of her lip when she hit the floor. Emotionally, I don't think she could cope with the ER."

They pulled into the garage and Bryce helped Ann out of the car. He then extended his hand to Asia as if she were a fine princess. She looked up into his face for the first time. She saw kindness there. It was something she had never seen in a man before. She decided to trust him...a little bit.

Ann did her best to get some information out of this somber, young lady as she took a closer look at Asia's nose and lip. She would, no doubt, be sore and bruised for a few days, but otherwise she was uninjured.

Ann tried to read the girl's eyes; eyes filled with hopelessness, pain and deep sorrow. She recognized that look. Not only did she recognize it, she had felt it herself...years ago...before Bryce. *Something more serious is going on than just what happened today*, Ann thought

This girl is petrified, Bryce thought as he patted her arm.

"Everything is going to be all right," he assured her.

Ann knew by the quiver of her chin that Asia wasn't so sure this was true. She was pretty sure Asia understood a bit more than she was able to speak; after all she did have a job that required at least some minimal communication. Ann gently washed the dried blood and tear stains from the girl's face.

I'm sure she lives somewhere in town and she must walk to work. I don't recall ever seeing her get in or out of a car. If she refuses to talk to me, how can I help her?

Chapter 24

I
t was past lunch time, so Ann turned on the stove and began preparing soup and sandwiches. *Asia might be able to handle some soup.*

Bryce planted a kiss on Ann's cheek before taking down bowls, plates and glasses to set the table.

Asia watched Bryce as he moved around the kitchen. She saw how he smiled at his wife. He never missed an opportunity to touch her or hug her. She had never witnessed this kind of behavior before. It intrigued her.

She tried to be inconspicuous with her observations. *He acts like he...LOVES her! Could that be true?*

Ann was surprised when Asia appeared at her elbow, picked up the plate of sandwiches and sat it on the table. She took the water pitcher from Bryce and filled the glasses.

When everything was ready Bryce pulled out Ann's chair. Then he did the same for Asia. Her confused look revealed much about how she was accustomed to being treated. It was also obvious by the way she attacked her food, even with a sore lip, that she had not eaten recently.

As the table was being cleared after lunch, Ann asked Asia if she could do makeup as well as hair. She nodded yes. Then Ann asked if she could sew and she pantomimed sewing to make sure Asia understood. She vigorously shook her head yes.

"We need someone with your skills to work at the Vincenzo Ballroom. Do you know where that is?" Ann asked. "Would you consider leaving the beauty shop and coming to work for us?"

Asia stared at Ann for several seconds before answering. "Yes, know where is. Yes, happy come work nice lady."

"That's wonderful Asia. When can you start?" Ann responded as she put the last of the silverware away and hung up the dishtowel.

"I start now," was her immediate response.

Like Victor and Anika, Asia was more than willing to earn her way. She wasn't afraid of work and was eager to start.

"Oh, no Asia, Wednesday is when our work week starts. For now, I want you to rest. You will be plenty sore by tomorrow as a result of your fall. I want to make sure you're okay," Ann said with a smile.

After Bryce finished wiping off the table, he came over to stand behind Ann. He wrapped his arms around her waist and rested his chin on her shoulder. Asia looked away.

"You can stay with us until you decide what you want to do permanently. Do you have belongings we need to pick up, or someone we need to contact about your change of address?" Bryce asked her, never raising his voice.

He knew intuitively that she was afraid of him. He wondered why...what on earth had happened to her in her short life to make her so fearful? Based on Ann's past, he had a pretty good idea what inspired that level of weariness around men.

"I'll take care of notifying the beauty shop that you will no longer be employed there," he told her gently.

In fact, I'll take great pleasure in talking to the owner, Bryce thought.

Chapter 25

Before Asia had a chance to answer, a police car could be seen coming up the driveway. It was Luke. He usually didn't drive a squad car home. Ann wondered what was going on.

"It's Luke," Ann said with obvious pleasure, as she turned toward Asia. "Luke is our..."

The look on the poor girl's face stopped her mid-sentence.

The terror that was always bubbling just beneath the surface swept through Asia's mind. She looked around wildly for some place to hide, then crouched in the corner beside the refrigerator. She wrapped her arms around her knees and buried her face.

Bryce gave Ann a questioning look and went to the door. Ann hurried over to Asia and helped the terrified girl off the floor. She pulled out a chair at the table an Asia obediently sat down.

By the serious expression on Luke's face, Ann knew something was wrong; this wasn't just a social visit.

"What's going on, son?" Bryce asked as Ann got Luke a cup of coffee and some left-over chocolate cake.

"A Mr. Cho came into the station a while ago claiming someone had stolen his 'property.' He was very agitated and speaking in Chinese or something. He finally calmed down enough to tell us that his 'girl' had been taken from the beauty shop where she worked part time."

He had gone on to give a description of the girl. Upon checking at the beauty shop, Luke had discovered there had been a little "misunderstanding" and the girl had become distraught. She had left with the Petersons.

It had been explained to Mr. Cho that in America nobody "owned" anybody. People were not considered property. This prompted much loud jabbering and gesturing until the police chief himself came out of his office. Mr. Cho was assured that his claim would be investigated. Hence, Luke's visit.

No amount of coaxing could illicit any answers from Asia as to her predicament. She just shivered and sobbed. Ann gave Luke a questioning look and a shrug as she propelled Asia to the guest room where Tylenol was dispensed before Asia was tucked under the covers. As Ann brushed her hair back from her forehead, she tried to reassure the young woman she had nothing to fear.

Ann was wrong. Asia had good reason to be fearful.

Chapter 26

The first thing Luke did upon returning to the police station was run a background check on Asia Kim and also Mr. Hong Cho. Asia Kim came up clean, assuming that was her real name. Hong Cho had been too stupid to use an alias. His rap sheet was colorful, to say the least.

He had been arrested several times for drug possession and petty theft, serving short amounts of jail time. Of more interest was his recent connection to prostitution. He had allegedly been smuggling young Asian girls into the United States, where they were for sale to the highest bidder.

So far, there had never been enough evidence to make charges stick. Witnesses were too afraid to testify. He had apparently found a way to climb into the next tax bracket thinking his lucrative activities could continue unchecked in this off-the-beaten-path, small town.

With this information, Luke obtained a search warrant for Mr. Cho's residence. On the outside it looked like any other house on the block, with a well kept lawn and a small American-made car in the garage. The inside was another story entirely.

Huddled in the corner of a back closet were two very young little girls; both naked. No attempt had been made to hide the lewd magazines and pornographic pictures that were strewn on the coffee table in the living room. Luke as well as the other members of the search team, were sickened.

Child Services was called to take the little girls. If their parents could be found, they would be returned home. This small town police department had never been faced with anything of this magnitude. Even the chief was unsure about how to proceed. If the parents could not be found...well, they would cross that bridge when they came to it. In any case, Child Services would be responsible for them.

Mr. Cho was arrested. Now Luke definitely needed information from Asia Kim.

Luke returned to his parent's house later that evening. Over leftover meat loaf, he shared what he had learned. Asia sat stone-faced at the table as Luke asked her questions regarding her association with Hong Cho. The conversation was getting nowhere fast. Frustration grew with Asia's lack of cooperation.

Finally Ann took both of Asia's hand in hers and held them until the girl finally looked up at her.

"Asia, I know you're afraid. But you must understand that we can't help you unless you talk to us. I promise, you're not in trouble. Mr. Cho is in jail. He can't hurt you. We need to know about the little girls. We can't find their parents without your help. Do you know their names and where they are from?"

For several long seconds, Asia just stared at Ann. Finally, she said, "Not know real name of girls. Only know Sue and Linn. Names Cho give. Not know where parents."

Once she began telling her story, it all came spewing from her in great waves. What could be understood from her broken English, interspersed with her native tongue, was heart-wrenching.

Her father had sold her to, what sounded like, a broker of some sort, who in turn sold her to another man, who sold her to yet another man...and on it went all across the continent. She finally ended up with Mr. Cho.

She was from a fairly large city in southern China. The long, ghastly trip from city to city, man to man, until she finally arrived in this country, had nearly killed her. Her parents had not given her a name as they had only wanted a son. Asia Kim was what one of the men had called her. It's the only name she knew.

The two little girls were already in Mr. Cho's possession when Asia was brought to his house. She was told it was her job to look after them, making sure they were ready to receive "visitors."

She began to sob uncontrollably as she tried to explain what these "visitors" did to the little girls. When the little girls were finally unconscious, they had turned to her. They had used her in every horrible, inconceivable way. The beauty shop job was just a cover.

The details that were needed to make a case against Mr. Cho and find the others involved in this trafficking scheme, could only be obtained if Asia could communicate through an interpreter. Specific questions needed to be answered.

With what information Asia was able to provide, Luke felt he had enough to justify further time and money being spent in a broader investigation. The scope of this endeavor was too much for a small police department like Cedarville's to handle. Other government agencies would need to become involved. The FBI was called in. They promptly took over the case.

Chapter 27

D uring the search of Mr. Cho's house, nothing was found to prove that Asia or the other two girls were in this country legally. Child Services would deal with the children. Asia was older and if someone didn't intervene, she would be sent back to China. To what? A life on the streets or in a brothel?

One look at Ann's face told Bryce what was going through her mind. He saw her anguish. He knew she was remembering when she was a young girl, abused and alone. It's no wonder she wanted to help every waif who came across her path. It was one of the reasons he loved her so much.

Bryce called Oscar. They would need sound legal advice and also someone with resources and connections. Oscar didn't realize that Bryce had similar reasons for wanting to help Asia. It wasn't just because he loved Ann. His own past had been a painful one.

Attorney Oscar Schwartz, long time friend of Ann's, would deal with immigration. He would file the appropriate paperwork in order for Asia to stay and work in this country. The Petersons would gladly be her sponsors or guardians or whatever was needed to make this happen. He would also find someone who spoke Cantonese, which probably wouldn't be as easy as it had been to find someone who spoke Russian.

In the meantime, Asia was taken to meet Mama and Georgio. They, of course, immediately made her a part of the family. Instead of staying with Bryce and Ann, she decided she wanted to take Glo's old room, and start her new job.

She quickly picked up the routine of the nights the restaurant/ballroom was open. She seemed to understand what was needed to maintain the dance costumes along with her other responsibilities of hair and makeup.

Mama's hair had never looked better. Maria's new makeup complimented her dark complexion and eyes. Asia also wasn't shy about telling Bobby and Victor when they needed a trim. Everyone loved her.

Asia gravitated toward Victor and Anika and Bobby and Maria, who were closer to her in age. Bobby's constant teasing and exaggerated compliments had her blushing scarlet until Maria told her to think nothing of it. He was just a big boob sometimes.

"Bobby is boob?" Asia questioned.

Something must have gotten lost in translation because her puzzled expression brought on a deluge of laughter from Luke and Victor.

Bryce was trying very hard not to laugh as he buried his face in Ann's hair. Anika and Maria began giggling, which elicited chuckling from Georgio. The cascade effect soon had everyone laughing until Georgio was wiping tears from his eyes with his big, white hankie.

"Not to worry, Asia," Victor said between gasps for air. "I make much mistake when I come first to America too."

"Like you never make a mistake now," Bobby wheezed between snorts, as he tried to catch his breath.

Luke loved it.

"Yep. It's true. Bobby's a boob alright and Victor's English is perfect," he roared.

Finally realizing no one was laughing at her, Asia began to giggle, which only encouraged more laughing from the rest of the family.

"Asia, you'll have to get use to this kind of behavior," Georgio loudly whispered as he waved wildly at the boys. "These guys, they never stop!"

Mama clucked her tongue.

"It's a good thing Carla and John aren't here! Little JB would have been petrified at all this nonsense," she said sternly, before she dissolved into laughter again.

From then on, Asia felt accepted as part of the family.

Chapter 28

One of the older officers on the Cedarville police force was retiring, leaving a full time position open. Budget constraints and "politics" pushed the position to part time, opposite Luke who also worked part time.

The city officials were very proud of themselves for having acquired essentially full time police coverage for no benefits. In this small town, they made the rules, no matter how self-serving they were. Of course, they kept their high salaries and other benefits, including nice cars and lavish vacations.

Luke contacted his friend, Bruce Watson, who was still working at the Hudson County Sheriff's Department with the K9 Unit. After some thought and Luke's persistent urging, he decided to apply for the job.

It was half the pay without the insurance. Oh well. He was sick to death of bigger city crime and crap. He also hated small town pettiness and territorialism. He despised the stupid, insensitive people who always managed to be the ones in charge.

Most of them had absolutely no common sense. They had no idea about what was really going on or what needed to be done to solve the problems involving their community. He had to decide which he hated more. It was pretty much a toss-up.

If necessary, he had no problem telling people exactly how stupid they were and to hell with the consequences. He had a few reprimands in his jacket; so what? He was a really good cop. He was also the only K-9 officer with experience in the whole county. At least in Cedarville he would work with someone he liked and respected.

He liked Luke, finding him to be trustworthy and honest; qualities Bruce greatly admired, not finding them in too many people. He had had buddies in the Marine Corp, however, that was then and this was now. He lived simply without spending much, so this arrangement suited him until something better came along. He took the job and moved to a small apartment in Cedarville.

What a nothing little town, he thought as he drove down the quiet street leading to the police station. *I guess I won't have to worry about much excitement happening here.*

Chapter 29

One day, Luke was just getting off his shift when Bruce showed up early to catch up on paperwork. They decided to grab some lunch at a local hot dog stand.

As luck would have it, Bryce and Ann had acquired a taste for hot dogs that very same day; something they almost never ate. They were sitting at one of the outdoor tables when Luke and Bruce stepped up to the counter. They ordered six hot dogs each with monster shakes and a whole bag of cookies. Turning around, Luke spotted his parents immediately.

"Hey, looks who's here. Come on, let me introduce you to my parents," he said to Bruce as he began walking toward them, not waiting for a response.

Oh, this is just great, Bruce thought to himself. *Luke is always talking about what great parents he has. Now I'm going to have to suffer through eating my lunch with them! They're rich, live on a frigging estate for crying out loud and they own a fancy restaurant/ballroom kind of place, plus a manufacturing company! They're probably snobs.* He was prepared not to like them.

Mrs. Peterson was petite and attractive. When Luke introduced them she shook his hand warmly without a hint of any prejudice... or fear. Bruce was used to one or the other response when meeting new people.

Mr. Peterson stood, also shook his hand as he invited both men to join them. Bruce was reserved, but polite. He made no attempt to hide his frank scrutiny of the people Luke bragged about so much.

She was a real lady, exuding femininity from every pore. He could see the beginnings of laugh lines around her eyes and maybe a streak or two of white in her curls, but it was hard to guess her age. Her vivid blue eyes were frequently turned toward her husband. There was certainly no mistaking how she felt about him.

Luke's father was tall, thin and bald. Just an ordinary guy. But there was something about him. He had an attitude, a confidence or something, that gave him a certain open, appealing quality. He asked questions that were conversational without being intrusive.

Bruce had never seen two people, especially married to each other, who were so incredibly considerate of one another. They acted like newlyweds!

They must be married, what, at least twenty-some years. I'm a good five years older than Luke. Scowling slightly, he tried to do the math. *I wonder how old they really are? They sure seem to be smitten with each other!*

Asking if Luke or Bruce wanted anything more, Ann got up to get Bryce a refill on his drink, which he protested.

"You sit," he insisted. "I can get it myself."

Kissing him on the cheek she told him to relax and visit with the boys.

Bryce gave her his wallet and off she went to the counter.

If anyone else had made that "boys" comment in any other setting, Bruce would have taken immediate offense. Somehow, right now, right here, it just made him feel...included. He wasn't sure if he liked it or not. A second thought followed. *He trusts his wife with his wallet? What a fool!*

Bryce watched Ann walk to the counter. His eyes never left her. Luke watched Bruce, watch Bryce, watch his mother. The incredulous look on his friend's face struck Luke as highly amusing. He was unsuccessful at controlling the chuckle that was rising in his chest and was soon laughing out loud.

Luke slapped Bruce on the back.

"Hey man, you better get use to how they are together. They're like that all the time."

Ann set the drink down in front of Bryce, then took her seat next to him, patting his knee.

"Okay, what did I miss that was so funny?"

"Oh, nothing Mom. Bruce here, he isn't quite used to you and Dad yet."

Ann handed over the change and her husband's wallet.

"Thanks, sweetie," Bryce whispered.

The rest of lunch was, thankfully, uneventful for Bruce; he did however continue to watch them covertly.

Bryce and Ann stood up and began gathering their belongings.

"Bruce, why don't you come Friday evening for dinner at Vincenzo's? Be our guest. You do like Italian food don't you?" Bryce said.

There was an awkward pause as Bruce was taken off guard by this invitation.

Realizing his discomfort, Ann gave Bruce a friendly smile.

"It was a pleasure to meet you Bruce. We hope to see you Friday."

He mumbled something unintelligible and nodded, hoping it passed for a refusal, all the time thinking, *What is up with these people? They can't be for real.*

Chapter 30

Ann was quiet as they drove home. Bryce knew she was thinking about Bruce. She had found another "little" fledgling that needed mothering. He smiled. *My little wife has a heart for anyone lost or hurting.*

Friday night arrived and Bruce wasn't going to go to dinner at Vincenzo's. *I'll feel like a duck out of water. It's ridiculous! Who am I kidding?* But somehow, there he was, pulling into the parking lot at seven-thirty sharp, dressed in his best suit.

As soon as he walked in, he was suddenly surrounded by a group of people all waiting to shake his hand. Bryce parted the group like Moses parted the Red Sea and came to his rescue. Bobby and Maria, John and Carla, Victor and Anika, Georgio and Mama Rosa were introduced and enthusiastically welcomed this newcomer to the fold.

Bruce looked uncomfortable and slightly overwhelmed. Being a solitary man, he wasn't use to being the center of so much attention. The group moved en mass to a large round table with a reserved placard in the center. This was the family's table. A place had been set for him...just in case.

The food was delicious and plentiful. *Maybe this wasn't such a bad idea after all,* he decided after his second helping of lasagna.

He was bombarded with questions from all sides, which he tried to answer between mouthfuls. Yes, he liked living in Cedarville. No, he wasn't married. The food was great, and yes, he was getting all he wanted. Yes, he could just barely tolerate working with Luke, "the big lug."

In any other situation, he would have considered Bobby a punk. As the evening wore on, he realized all the kidding around was out of fun. Bobby and Luke were more like brothers. Deep down, he envied that relationship.

He wasn't sure how Victor and Anika fit into the group. Anika called Bryce and Ann something that sounded like Mama and Papa. They obviously hadn't been in the United States long. Their English wasn't too bad; they were easily understood. *Victor has the potential to be as obnoxious as Bobby,* Bruce thought as he ate this second cannoli, *but he seems like an okay guy.*

Carla and John. Now there was another anomaly. They definitely were not related biologically to anyone at this table. They talked a lot about little JB, who Bruce assumed was their son. It was also evident that everyone adored the kid, especially Mr. and Mrs. Vincenzo.

Chapter 31

Suddenly, during a lull in the conversation, a woman screamed. The whole room went silent for just a heartbeat. Then murmurs could be heard rippling from table to table. Some of the men stood, but were unsure what to do.

Luke and Bruce were immediately in motion. A second scream followed the first, sounding like it came from the hallway behind the stage.

Ann was terrified, every drop of color draining from her face. She knew instinctively what generated that kind of scream. She thought it sounded like Asia. Bryce quickly pulled her close. He knew exactly what she was thinking and his lips brushed her cheek.

"Ann, I want you to wait right here with Bobby. I'll be right back."

Asia never ate in the main dining room with the rest of the family. She preferred to work in the background, keeping out of sight. Ann understood her fear better than anyone else.

"Bobby, watch out for the girls. John, use the intercom and assure our guests that everything is under control."

Everyone did exactly as instructed. Bryce and Georgio hurried after Luke and Bruce.

Luke threw open the door to the hall in time to see Butch hurl himself through the air, landing heavily on a man who was mauling

Asia! Man and dog flew to the floor. A wrestling match ensued between the now terrified man and the big, ugly dog.

Having received some training after the last incident where Butch had rescued a damsel in distress, he now knew exactly what he was supposed to do and he did it with a fury!

Just before she fainted, Bruce caught Asia.

Despite the guy's best effort, he couldn't dislodge the massive jaws from his arm.

"Butch! Off," Luke commanded.

After a good shake of his head, causing the man to cry out in pain, Butch came obediently to Luke's side.

"Butch! Watch!"

Butch swung his big head toward the intruder, a low menacing growl rumbling in his chest.

Pushing himself to his feet and leaning against the wall, the man demanded someone call the police.

"I've been attached by a mad dog," he yelled, his wild eyes never leaving Butch.

The yelling stopped when Luke shoved his badge under the guy's nose.

"I AM the police. Just what do you think you're doing back here?"

Didn't I just do this same thing not long ago? Luke thought disgustedly. *This is exactly why I went into law enforcement; to protect innocent people from scum like this.*

Bryce and Georgio came through the door in time to hear Luke's question. Asia had "come to" and she was clinging to Bruce, her face buried in his neck. She looked like a fragile, little doll in the big man's arms and Bruce held her like she could easily break.

Chapter 32

Quickly assessing the situation, Bryce stuck his head out the door and motioned for Ann. He didn't know if Asia was injured or not. She was still holding tight to Bruce. The man was holding his arm as if it hurt. Bryce assumed Butch had something to do with that.

Chester Spencer was handcuffed after Ann made sure he wasn't hurt; just scared. Bryce brought a chair and Bruce sat Asia down, kneeling protectively beside her. She was such a delicate, little thing. Bruce had a hard time catching his breath as he looked at her.

Ann turned her attention to Asia.

"Honey, what on earth happened?" Are you hurt?"

"Not hurt, Butch save. Know man from Mr. Cho. He come many time. Do bad thing to me and other girls," Asia said in hushed tones as she reached for Bruce and held tight to his hand.

As afraid of men as Asia was, her fear didn't seem to extend to Bruce and he was a pretty scary-looking, big guy. The anger on his face wasn't directed at Asia and he continued to talk calmly and quietly to her.

Luke radioed for a squad car to come and pick up Mr. Spencer, who was already yelling that he wanted a lawyer.

I'll be darned. Didn't know Bruce had a tender side, Luke thought, observing his friend with Asia.

Not to be excluded, Butch pushed his way in beside Asia. He sat whining, his jowls resting on her knee, his sad brown eyes watching her face.

Mr. Spencer was charged with assault. When the police car arrived, the officers spoke briefly with Luke, then marched the prisoner out the back door so as not to cause any more disruption of the evening.

As the arresting officer, Luke would follow to complete the paperwork. Other charges would probably follow, associated with Mr. Spencer's activities at Cho's establishment.

Asia finally let go of Bruce's hand and bowed her head.

"Thank you most honorable sir for help Asia," she whispered without looking up.

"Asia, this is Officer Bruce Watson. He's a friend of the family," Ann said softly to Asia. "Bruce, this is Asia Kim. She lives and works here at Vincenzo's."

"I'm sorry to have to meet you under these circumstances ma'am," Bruce replied gently.

Ann looked from Bruce to Asia, her mind whirring with possibilities.

Chapter 33

Bryce called an emergency family meeting for the following morning to discuss the events that had transpired the night before. It had become obvious that Peterson Enterprise, including Vincenzo's Restaurant & Ballroom, would need to beef up security. Asia would continue to be in danger and then there was always Ann's past to take into consideration.

A suggestion was made to ask Bruce if he would like to fill out his part time job at the police station by working part time for Vincenzo's providing additional security. Luke also decided to stop by the animal shelter on a regular basis to try and find another teachable, good-sized dog. Butch had certainly proven his worth... twice!

There had been no serious injuries to Asia unless you consider being scared to death an injury. It was decided to leave Butch with her unless he was specifically needed in a police-related situation.

From then on, everywhere Asia went, Butch could be seen following at her heels. He even slept by her bed at night. She drew the line when he wanted to sleep ON the bed. The smile on her face was proof that she felt much safer under the dog's supervision.

Bryce asked Bruce to stop by the restaurant.

"We would like to offer you a part time position working here at Vincenzo's," Bryce began. "We all feel the need for heightened security for reasons which will be further explained to you if you accept the position. I want you to also know that the decision to ask you to consider joining us was a unanimous one."

John went over the salary, insurance benefits and retirement package, asking Bruce if he had any questions. Bruce was dumbfounded by the generous offer. He couldn't have thought of a question if his life depended on it!

Victor explained how their usual evening schedule progressed through dinner and dancing. At eight-thirty all the couples began their rounds of each table as had become their habit from the reopening of the restaurant. Dancing began at nine o'clock sharp.

A black man is in charge of finances! A little Hispanic punk is second in command under Bryce and Georgio. A Russian is leader of the dance team and an Asian girl has the responsibility of how everyone looks. His mind raced as Bruce looked around the table trying to get a grasp of where everyone fit into this unorthodox "family" and that's exactly what it was. A big family.

Everything about this whole setup amazed Bruce. He had been told if he accepted the position, everything would be further laid out for him at his first Wednesday Family Meeting. Bryce and Georgio said they understood if he wanted some time to think over their offer.

With a big smile on his face, Georgio shook his hand.

"Please let us know as soon as possible if you want the job. We all hope you choose to join us."

This has to be some kind of joke, Bruce decided on the drive back to his apartment. *It was too good to be true. None of the people he had ever known acted like this...well, except for Granny, God rest her soul. And Asia! What the hell!* Just before falling asleep that night, he decided to accept the position.

Chapter 34

Bruce Watson had grown up in Brooklyn, NY. His mother had to work long hours to support him and his baby brother, leaving them with their grandmother a good share of the time. They had a very small apartment in the projects.

As Bruce grew older, the temptation to join one of the gangs was always nipping at his heels. His grandmother wanted something better for her favorite grandson, so she encouraged him to study hard and keep his nose clean.

He managed to graduate high school, after which he joined the Marine Corp. He was a big, black, tough kid and the rigors of military life suited him. He excelled. He was relatively happy for the first time in his life.

His Granny wrote to him every week. Her letters were always cheerful, never reflecting the dreary life she actually lived. He looked forward to reading them. Her letters were the only mail he ever got.

After boot camp, he came home on leave. He could see the pride in his grandmother's eyes when he walked in the door wearing his dress uniform. He hadn't been home twenty-four hours before his mother began complaining to him about his brother's behavior.

Unlike Bruce, Thad couldn't resist the lure of the gang. The money, the girls, the sex, the drugs... He was almost never home anymore; a source of constant worry for his mother.

"Can't you talk to him, Bruce? He might listen to you," his mother pleaded.

So Bruce did talk to his brother...to no avail.

The lack of change in Thad was, according to his mother, his fault. He was to blame. He hadn't been stern enough. He hadn't presented it in the right way... His mother went on and on in her whiney, irritating, nagging way until Bruce finally couldn't take it anymore. He headed out to the corner bar for a beer.

Sitting on a stool at the end of the bar, sipping morosely on his beer, Bruce didn't notice Tonya until she was perched next to him.

"Hey, big fella. Wanna buy a girl a drink?" she asked seductively, leaning just a little too close, showing just a little too much cleavage.

Why not? Bruce thought to himself. He was bored. He was down to his last few nights of leave for God's sake. He certainly didn't want to go home where his mother was waiting to pounce on him again.

After several drinks, one thing quickly led to another. In the morning he woke up in a strange apartment beside a still-sleeping, voluptuous, light-skinned girl. His memory was fuzzy. What had he done...exactly?

She awoke slowly, stretched and purred into his ear.

"That was wonderful, Baby. Let's do it again."

Before his leave was over, he and Tonya were married. He insisted to his mother and grandmother it was "love at first sight."

His mother was furious. His grandmother was disappointed. He figured they would both get over it. The look on his Granny's face bothered him a lot. He hated feeling like he had let her down somehow.

Before Bruce left for active duty, he and Tonya rented a little apartment. A bank loan would pay for the new furniture she wanted. He promised her he would be sending money home for the rent and other bills.

When his leave was over, she didn't want him to go. Pouting and cajoling, she clung to him. She didn't seem to understand he was a Marine and he had to follow orders.

"You don't have to worry about anything, sweetheart. Just wait for me. I love you!" Bruce said to her with a tremor in his voice.

Prying her arms from around his waist, he kissed her one last time. His flight to Germany was boarding. Last call.

Chapter 35

Over the next two years Bruce sent money to Tonya as promised, assuming all was well. He also started a savings account where he regularly socked money away toward a house. When he got out, he was looking forward to starting a family. Tonya said that's what she wanted too. He believed her. He trusted her.

He came home twice on short leaves before being sent to the Middle East. He spent as much time as he could visiting with his family. His mom was bitter about her lot in life. She began harping on him the minute he entered the house. His grandma looked older and more tired than he remembered. His brother was serving time for burglary and assault. No surprise there.

Tonya was always happy to see him each time he came home. They made passionate love all night and slept half the day. Bruce thought he was the luckiest man alive.

Every day, Bruce thought about Tonya and the life they would have together when he was discharged. He called her whenever he could. He wondered about the laughter he sometimes heard in the background. He tried not to think about it. He trusted her...

Chapter 36

He was hot and tired as his platoon trudged back toward the barracks after a day wasted tracking phantoms through the desert. It appeared their intelligence hadn't been accurate... again. The ambush came out of nowhere.

Two weeks later, Bruce woke up in the field hospital, half his face swathed in heavy bandages, his leg in traction and his head aching. He was told he had dragged two of his fellow Marines to safety. He had gone back for a third when he was hit. He was lucky to be alive. Several of his friends hadn't made it.

Now that he was conscious, he could be flown to Germany from the field hospital and from there, back to the United States. He would need rehabilitation when the traction came off his leg and probably plastic surgery for his face. But he was alive and going home with an honorable discharge, plus a couple of medals. He considered himself very lucky.

Headaches continued to plague him, along with the nightmares of his time in the desert. He survived by clinging to the vision he kept in his mind of Tonya waiting for him at the end of his long recovery.

The military had offered to fly her to Germany so she could be with him. He was shocked and a little hurt that she refused to come with some lame excuse about her job. He wondered why she wasn't as anxious to see him as he was to see her.

Finally the day came. He was going home. Bruce could hardly contain his excitement as his plane taxied to a stop at LaGuardia Airport. He had wired Tonya of his arrival. He assumed she would be there to meet him.

He limped off the plane, leaning heavily on his cane. He ignored the people who stared at the scar on his face. He didn't care what they thought about how he looked. He would soon be in his sweet Tonya's arms. That was the only thing that mattered to him.

He was disappointed when he couldn't find Tonya, even after having her paged. His disappointment turned to worry that something had happened to her. An accident, maybe, or a sudden illness.

More than a little upset, he took a cab from the airport to his apartment. When his key wouldn't open the door, he called for the super. Mr. Hayes was new to this building. He didn't know anyone named Tonya. Feeling sorry for a wounded veteran, he unlocked the door.

Bruce was stunned to see the apartment completely empty. The furniture, the appliances, even the curtains were gone. He got a sick feeling in the pit of his stomach as he headed out the door. She hadn't waited for him at all! She was gone!

His next stop was the bank. The loan for the furniture was six months in arrears. His savings account was wiped out. He was devastated. He couldn't go home to his mother and grandmother, he was too ashamed. He had made a mess of everything and now he was alone.

Finding a cheap hotel with rooms to rent for a day at a time, he paid for a week and climbed the stairs to the third floor. The filthy room was disgustingly musty-smelling. It didn't matter. Nothing mattered any more. He flung his duffle bag to the floor and fell on the bed, hurt and angry.

Sleep proved impossible. His mind seemed caught in endless circles. He ran each scenario over and over again focusing on what he should have, could have, would have done differently. Feeling helpless for the first time in his life, he finally got up and stumbled out into the street.

The bar at the end of the block was filled with people willing to buy a wounded vet a drink. He was soon drunk, morose and looking for a fight. The last thing he remembered was hitting some guy in the face. He woke up in his bed at the hotel having no idea how he got there.

Chapter 37

After spending a week in a drunken stupor he dragged himself to the bathroom he shared with nine other people. When it was finally his turn, there wasn't any hot water left for a shower.

That figures. I should have gotten up earlier, he berated himself. His head ached like someone had hit it with a sledge hammer and his mouth was as dry as cotton.

He shivered under the weak stream of ice cold water. He remembered too late that he had forgotten to bring a towel, so he pulled on dirty clothes over his still wet body. *Might as well have not bothered with the shower,* he thought, trying to keep his teeth from chattering.

Still shaky from lack of food and way too much to drink, he waited in line for his turn to use the pay phone.

His grandmother had always been an inspiration to Bruce. He just knew if anyone could help him, Granny could. She would give him a whole new perspective on his situation. Her letters had stopped suddenly, but he had attributed that to the haphazard mail delivery. Plus, he had been moved to a couple of different hospitals. He was sure his mail just hadn't caught up with him yet.

While he waited for the call to go through, he tried to think of a way to tell her all that had happened. He decided that just telling the truth was the best approach.

His mother answered the phone.

"So nice of you to call, Bruce," she said sarcastically. "Your grandmother died last month. I sent you a letter. What have you been doing all this time? Partying with your soldier buddies?"

Shocked and sick with grief, Bruce hung up the phone without responding. He couldn't think of anything to say. Obviously, Tonya hadn't bothered to pass along the information related to his injuries and extended recovery time. What did it matter? Granny was dead. He had no one.

With tears streaming down his face, Bruce stumbled down the stairs and out the door. He walked the streets for hours, his heart aching with his loss, his mind numb. He had forgotten his cane and his leg throbbed.

It started to rain just as he passed St. Michael's Catholic Church. The door was open. He was given a hot meal and a warm bed in the men's dorm. Father Cassidy proved to be a good listener and a good friend.

There was always work that needed to be done around the Parish. Bruce was glad for something constructive to do. He attended the services and spent time talking to the elderly priest. Finally, one day, he realized he was going to live after all.

It had been Father Cassidy's idea for Bruce to try for a job with the NYPD. His training in the Marine Corp made him an excellent candidate and he needed a job, a real job, so he applied.

Chapter 38

H is experience with the canine unit in the military was a plus for the police department. His talents were immediately put to good use upon graduation from the academy.

The dog assigned to him was unimpressive. He didn't have the instincts or the drive of the dogs Bruce had worked with in the past. The dog was finally given to another officer as a pet for his kids, a task for which this particular dog was eminently qualified to do.

Bruce was given several different dogs, all of which were satisfactory. None of which ever truly bonded with him. It became just boring work.

After two years with the K-9 unit in the Bronx, Bruce wanted out of the big city with its greed and corruption at the highest levels of city government. He started looking for opportunities in smaller cities.

The Hudson County Police Academy in Freeport, VT was looking for an instructor to develop a K-9 training program. He thought about it for at least sixty seconds before he took vacation time and made the trip to Vermont. He submitted an application along with his resume and was interviewed.

He was hired on the spot. He returned to New York, resigned his position, gathered his few belongings and headed back to Vermont.

Classes would run for eight weeks. Every officer was to bring his own dog and students would be accepted from several surrounding counties. Bruce was strict. With his size and demeanor, he made sure the students followed his instructions exactly. His expectations were high. Only the best students graduated. Only the committed would succeed.

Several classes had graduated, with well-trained officers taking spots in police departments all over the area. Bruce was considered one of the best instructors in the academy.

Part of his success was his ability to intimidate his students with just one glare. He used his "best" feature to his advantage. He didn't want to be anybody's "buddy" or anybody's "mommy."

A new group had been assembled in the training yard behind the courthouse. Bruce stood with his arms crossed over his bulging chest, his feet apart, his hat pulled low on his brow as he observed this new group of young officers and their dogs.

One officer and his dog stood out from the rest. One reason being the size of the dog who didn't back away when Bruce leaned over him to perform a cursory examination.

When he was introduced to handler, Officer Luke Peterson, he was impressed when the young man's eyes never wavered from his. *Okay, this is more like it*, he thought to himself as he continued down the line.

When Luke graduated from the program, he and Bruce kept in touch. Luke contacted him occasionally with questions regarding handing a specific situation and Bruce was always a good source of information.

Over time, a friendship developed.

Chapter 39

Oscar had worked miracles in a short period of time on Asia's behalf. She was granted permission to stay and work in the United States. Everyone was very relieved, especially Ann. She had been so worried about losing one of her "children."

Through the interpreter, Asia had spoken with the FBI regarding Mr. Cho and what she knew about his operation, which wasn't much. She had been passed from person to person, never knowing names or places. Her testimony did, however, put Mr. Cho in prison, which was exactly where he belonged.

He offered to give information regarding the people higher up the food chain, in return for a reduced sentence. Oscar wasn't in favor of this arrangement. The guy deserved the maximum possible sentence.

Disgruntled, he was forced to accept the fact that it was out of his control. The investigation was ongoing with the understanding that Asia may be called sometime in the future to give her testimony yet again.

Asia was more at ease knowing Mr. Cho was safely behind bars. She still preferred not to come to the dining room on work nights. The very next man through the door might be someone who "knew" her. Her fear and shame ran deep.

The parents of the two little girls had not been found, which didn't surprise Asia. People in her country didn't want girls. Sue and

Linn had been placed together in a foster home where they were well cared for and happy. When the specified time had passed and the investigation was completed, the childless couple wanted to adopt the little girls.

Chapter 40

After Bruce accepted the security position, he was brought up to speed regarding Asia's background, as well as Ann's. He couldn't be part of the team without knowing all the facts. He understood that he was one of only a few people who were privy to Ann's witness protection status.

If he had opinions about what he was told, he never mentioned them. He kept a close eye on Asia, knowing Bryce would be keeping an eye on Ann. Bruce began spending a lot of time with Asia, even when he wasn't "working."

It wasn't long before they were good friends. She became a more open and confident young lady. Bruce, in turn, was softening around the edges. He had even smiled once, according to Georgio.

When Bruce wasn't with her, Asia never left Vincenzo's. He took the graveyard shift at the police department so that he could spend more time with her.

He seemed to be thriving in his new job as "bodyguard." That's what Luke and Bobby called him. He took the kidding in stride while doubling up his big fists and flexing his huge biceps. He would give them his meanest stare; a tactic which always brought a cascade of giggles from Asia.

As time went by, Bruce and Asia fell in love. It was a wonderful thing to watch and it was a privilege to witness the journey. Asia became a friendly, vivacious young woman. Bruce took on a gentle quality with her that was heartwarming. He was helping her study to take the exam that would make her a citizen.

"I not marry Bruce until American Citizen," Asia confided to Ann, a shy smile on her round face. "I make proud."

A small beauty shop had been added to restaurant/ballroom along the back hall beside the dressing rooms and snack bar. Asia could now easily do hair and makeup without having to use her own room. No expense was spared. She had two chairs and two sinks, along with everything she would need to make everyone look their best.

Mama had a couple of friends her age who didn't like going to the beauty shop in Cedarville so Asia offered to do their hair. Soon she was getting more customers from the community and giving the shop in town a run for their money.

"It's just what they deserve," Bobby said, shaking his head in disgust at the behavior of such prejudiced people.

Chapter 41

Carla and John were expecting another baby. Everyone was so happy for this young couple who had thought they would never have children. Ann had referred them to a clinic that specialized in the reproductive problems that plagued many disabled men. The success rate for this clinic was high and they had become the parents of Little JB, John Bryce.

Georgio stroked his mustache.

"A little girl would be nice this time," he hinted with a grin.

"I did my best," John laughed. "Now that we've got the hang of this whole baby thing, we want to have a lot of them!"

His wheelchair didn't matter anymore. He had a great job that he loved working with a group of wonderful people who were like family to him. He had a beautiful wife and he was about to be a father for the second time. He was indeed a happy man.

They currently lived in a two bedroom apartment in Cedarville and with the new baby coming, they would need more room. Since Peterson Enterprise had expanded and owned the land from Vincenzo's almost all the way to Cedarville, it was decided at a family meeting to build John and Carla a house.

"Why don't we just build a couple of houses on a little cul de sac?" Luke suggested. "Bobby and Marie have been wanting a house of their own and will eventually get around to having kids. And heck, who knows? I might even want one someday. A kid, that is."

"Does Tess have anything to say about this?" Georgio interjected innocently.

"Oh, brother," Luke moaned. "I should have kept my mouth shut. Bobby, don't you dare repeat anything I just said to Tess, or you will not live long enough to regret it!"

"Luke, is there something you want to tell us?" Ann asked, with a huge smile on her face.

"No, no, Mom. I don't think Tess sees me as a prospective... mate," was Luke's dejected response.

For now, Victor and Anika were satisfied living in one of the Vincenzo apartments. It gave them easy access to the ballroom where they practiced and worked on new routines. They were completely dedicated to dancing. No time for children now. Besides they were still young. There would be lots of time to start a family.

The new houses would free up Bobby and Maria's apartment for Bruce and Asia when they decided to get married. This worked perfectly for Bruce as he was responsible for security over everything on the "Vincenzo" side of the road. This included the restaurant/ballroom, Georgio and Mama's apartment and the new houses to be built up the road.

The opposite side of the road would be Luke's responsibility. It included the Peterson Estate, the parking lot/garage, cars/limos and the soon-to-be completed Goodwin-Schwartz Free Clinic.

Ann was thrilled that her vision for a health care clinic was coming to fruition. The clinic would house two treatment rooms, two patient rooms, a supply room, an office and a lobby with a reception desk. Tess was going to join Ann in the practice and as promised, Bryce was going to man the reception desk.

Bobby found the idea of Bryce being a "secretary" hilarious and he never lost an opportunity to poke fun.

"Are you going to wear a cute little outfit? Will you be learning shorthand? How about typing?" Bobby taunted.

Bryce took it all in stride with a smile.

"Whatever the boss wants," he answered, wrapping his arms around Ann and nuzzling her neck. "Absolutely anything she wants."

Chapter 42

The Vincenzo Ballroom Dance Team was getting ready for their first major competition. They would be dancing against teams from all over the state. Victor and Anika were in an absolute frenzy. They took the responsibility as leaders of the team very seriously.

This was their big chance to make or break the reputation of the team. They didn't want to let the family down, although Georgio kept trying to assure them that all would be well whether they won or lost.

"Aw, man!" Bobby complained. "Do we have to go over this step again?" We've already done it at least a million times."

"Go over until perfect," was Victor's reply. "You want win, yes? All must be perfect."

Bryce was surprised when Victor asked if they could have a meeting with the wait staff and the kitchen help. No matter how curious he was, he didn't ask any questions, he just scheduled the meeting.

When the restaurant had reopened, the employees involved with all areas of food preparation and service had been asked to decide on the styles and colors of the uniforms they wanted. They had decided on classic black and white.

When everyone was assembled, Victor asked if they minded if the dance team also wore black and white with variations in styles and patterns. It would be the signature colors for the ballroom as well as the dance team. Everyone was shocked that Victor even asked for their permission and opinions.

"We want look unique. Same as restaurant. People know by see... how you say...we all represent Vincenzo's by our look alike."

"Nicely put," Bobby laughed as he punched Victor's arm. "We get it."

Bryce was proud of Victor. He had learned how to inspire loyalty and cooperation, or maybe it wasn't so much that he had learned how important this was, he was just treating people the way he wanted to be treated himself.

He had elevated the morale of the ancillary staff. They, in turn, took pride in being part of the Vincenzo Team. No one part of the team was more important than any other part. The busboys were just as necessary to the success of the team as the dancers and the leadership.

Chapter 43

C laire Lafontaine was busy trying to come up with different costumes for each dance using only black and white. It was a challenge, but the end result was worth the effort. There was no mistaking they all represented Vincenzo's Restaurant and Ballroom.

Victor had made inquiries, gathering information on how the state-wide competitions were organized. He wanted to make sure they weren't disqualified because they didn't follow the rules. At a family meeting several weeks before the event, he had gone over everything that would be expected.

Everyone was nervous on the day of the competition; even Georgio and Mama. After all, it had been many years since they had danced competitively in a venue this size against already established teams. The only one who was not worried about performing was Bobby.

"Yo, guys. We've got this in the bag. No worries," he assured them.

Since Luke didn't dance, he would be acting as chauffeur. Bruce would handle any safety or security problems that arose.

"I don't want my new limo to end up wrapped around a telephone pole with one of you guys driving," Luke kidded.

To everyone's surprise, Asia appeared holding Bruce's hand.

"If problem with dress, need sew, I there fix," was her simple explanation.

The smile on her face was like a breath of fresh air, as Bruce helped her into the waiting limo. She was truly happy; a new experience for her. The big man, in full dress tuxedo, climbed in after her.

John, Carla and Tess came along for moral support. It had not been easy to find a babysitter for JB. She had to be perfect, after all, to satisfy everyone. They wouldn't think of leaving their pride and joy with just anybody. But Missy, a teen volunteer at the hospital, well known to Tess, fit the bill. JB loved her immediately.

There was only one not present and accounted for and that was Butch. Mama wouldn't have been surprised to find him in the front seat with Luke. She was also pretty sure Bobby would have found a reasonable explanation for why he needed to be there.

Chapter 44

U pon arrival at the competition venue, TV cameras were everywhere, filming each group as they arrived. When the Vincenzo team stepped out of their limo, they looked like they had been doing this for years.

All of the teams were welcomed to the first ballroom dance competition of the season.

"Welcome dance teams and spectators," the announcer began. "Everyone, please find your places. The dancing will begin in just a few minutes."

As the announcer continued reciting the rules of the judging, the order of the dances etc. the Vincenzo team went to the area assigned to them to do last minute makeup and clothing adjustments. They were ready to perform.

"Ladies and Gentleman, the first dance of tonight's competition will be the Cha Cha Cha. Dancers, please take your places."

Each couple was assigned a number, which was attached to the back of the man's coat or shirt and they were introduced as they stepped onto the floor. The judging would be done as they danced in their appropriate group. Each couple would receive a score and the highest score won the dance.

"It's time to show 'um what we got," Bobby laughed as he took Maria's hand and led her onto the floor.

Bobby and Maria would also dance the Samba and the Mambo. Unfortunately, they didn't place in any of them.

Victor and Anika danced the Quick Step, Tango and the Jive. They placed third in the Quick Step.

"Victor's mother would be so proud," Ann murmured to Bryce.

The next dance was the Fox Trot. All the participants were announced.

"From the Vincenzo Ballroom in Cedarville, Georgio and Rosa Vincenzo."

There were tears in Ann's eyes when Mama and Georgio took their places. With all the exercise involved with practice, both had slimmed down. Asia had worked her magic and Mama looked beautiful. Her silver hair swept up, her black sequined gown falling to her ankles. Georgio strutted his stuff in a black tuxedo, his hair and mustache neatly trimmed. They made a handsome couple.

Two of the older judges looked up from their judging forms when they heard the name Vincenzo. Apparently, they were familiar with the European Latin and Ballroom Champions. A knowing look passed between them. This would be a team to watch!

It was no surprise when Georgio and Rosa won first place. Georgio had a smug smile, while Mama blushed like a schoolgirl when the ribbons were awarded.

The Waltz was the last dance of the evening. Bryce and Ann took their places.

"Are you nervous?" Bryce whispered.

Ann looked up into his face. Her eyes sparkled with excitement. "Not when I'm with you, my love."

They were a stunning couple. Ann in a long, white gown, the bodice covered in sequins. Her long, curly hair held away from her face with a diamond-studded clip.

Bryce was an attractive man in his white tuxedo. Together, they made a very eye-catching couple. They exuded romance. Every woman in the room wished she was Ann. Every man wished he was Bryce.

When the music ended, the spectators were immediately on their feet, clapping wildly. Bryce and Ann were oblivious. Bryce pressed a kiss to her palm. They did not place, but they didn't care. They were happy.

This was the first competition of the season and usually favorites had not yet been chosen by dance enthusiasts who followed the competitions. The Vincenzo team was ecstatic when Bryce and Ann got a standing "O." That just didn't happen.

It usually took years to build a fan base. Jimmy had been right. They had that special "something." A quality everyone wanted, but few had. People really DID love watching them dance.

They celebrated all the way home.

"Those judges just don't know a good Cha Cha when they see it," Bobby complained. "We'll get 'um next time, Baby," he said to Maria, hugging her close.

Victor pointed out their loss was probably due to his "two left foots and horrible posture."

It had been great fun though and now they knew where they stood when compared to other dancers. Victor was already evaluating their weak spots.

Bruce just shook his head.

"Hey punk," he called to Bobby over the din of the celebrating. "Do I have to show you how it's done?"

Everyone laughed. Especially Bobby.

Now the real work began.

Chapter 45

"Dad! Turn on the local news. You won't believe this! We have a real problem!"

It had been a late night for the dance team. Bryce and Ann were still in bed the next morning when they got the frantic call from Luke. Bryce was thinking along an entirely different line as he drew patterns with his fingertip on his wife's bare shoulder. Luke made it sound important so he flipped on the TV in the bedroom.

Channel Nine News had just started a story on the opening of the dance season in the Hudson County area. Danielle Sullivan was doing a story covering the highlights of the competition, giving results and general information on this year's schedule.

She concluded her piece by saying, "A surprising highlight of the evening was the Peterson and Peterson couple from the Vincenzo Ballroom in Cedarville. This husband and wife team sprang up out of nowhere to capture the hearts of everyone watching, receiving the first standing ovation of the season. As you watch our final clip, it is easy to see why some are already calling them the 'King and Queen of Romance.' This new team is led by former European Ballroom and Latin dance champions, Georgio and Rosa Vincenzo. And that's our broadcast for this evening. Stay tuned to Channel Nine, reporting all that's new, all the time."

Behind the credits as they scrolled up the screen was a clip of Bryce and Ann dancing their very beautiful Waltz. They both bolted upright in bed, their eyes popping.

The phone rang again. It was Luke.

"Apparently, this wasn't the first run of this story because we have already gotten a call from Channel Nine News wanting to do a live feature story on our dance team! Bobby and Marie have been taking reservations since we turned the phones on this morning. Everyone is clamoring to see 'Mr. and Mrs. Romance!' Dad, what are we going to do? This could put Mom in serious danger!"

"We're getting up right now. Your mother and I will be at the restaurant in an hour. We need to discuss this situation with the rest of the family."

No time for their usual love-making and leisurely shower this morning. Plans needed to be made and put into motion ASAP!

Chapter 46

I n a seedy, rent-by-the-week, or by the hour, flea-infested, rat-trap of a motel on the outskirts of Boston, wearing only his dirty underwear and morosely slurping the last beer in the six pack, another individual bolted upright, suddenly sober as a judge.

There, in fuzzy black and white on his stolen TV was a face he recognized even after twenty years. How could he forget? She had changed his world forever and he hated her with everything in him. Having lost his most recent job, in a series of many lost jobs, it seemed his luck was about to change for the better.

It's all her fault, the little bitch, he thought to himself as he sat penniless in this stinky room with cockroaches as his only friends. *Her fault! I'll get even if it's the last thing I do. And I know just the person to call to get the job done.*

As he dialed the number from the public phone in the hall, his lips twisted in a nasty, contorted smile.

"Hey," he barked into the receiver when his call was answered. "Do you want in on a plan to make some serious money? I'll split the money with you after expenses. My only condition is that I get the girl."

"How much money are we talking?" was the response.

"I'm not sure exactly. Do you know anything about a Bryce Peterson or a Vincenzo's Restaurant?"

"Meet me at the bar on Clinton Street in an hour. We'll discuss it." was the enthusiastic reply. "I don't want to talk about this on the phone. And keep your mouth shut to anyone else or you know what will happen to you."

Chapter 47

Every face around the Vincenzo table was tight with worry. They were all aware of Ann's witness protection status. Now that her face had been on national television, her cover was blown.

They could only hope what had happened so long ago had been forgotten. Bryce doubted that. It had been a high profile case with two police officers and a well known contractor found guilty on all charges. They couldn't take the chance someone wouldn't want revenge.

"Let's not jump to conclusions," Bryce said with a calmness he didn't necessarily feel. "Nothing may come of this, but we should be prepared, just in case."

After carefully listening to everything Bryce said, Bruce asked a few questions regarding the whereabouts of Maynard Lewis, Art Dawson and Willie Thompson. "Unknown" wasn't the answer he wanted to hear.

"The first thing we need to do is find out where these guys are now," Luke began. "Bobby, why don't you use all that computer savvy you have and see if you can track them down. Bruce can access police records from the station. We will surely find some of the information we need there. Georgio, use your charm to get us out of doing that interview with Channel Nine News. Don't worry, Mom. We aren't going to let anything happen to you."

"What can rest of us to do?" Victor asked, his face serious.

"Be vigilant," Bryce said as he held Ann close. "We need to keep to our usual schedule and remain calm. Keep an eye out for anyone asking too many questions or anything that looks out of the ordinary. We can get together again tomorrow, hopefully with the information we need to proceed with a formal plan of action."

Ann shuddered. She alone knew exactly what these men were capable of doing. As much as her family loved her, she wasn't sure they could protect her from these evil people. Art had bragged that he had friends everywhere. He could get her no matter where she went. Her stomach began to churn.

Another dog needed to be found and trained for protection as soon as possible. Perhaps Hudson County had one they could spare until Luke could find one of his own.

Lewis shouldn't be hard to find. He hadn't gotten prison time, just bankrupted. Thompson had been sent to jail, but because of his cooperation he had received a lesser sentence and was probably paroled by now. Updated pictures of them would be obtained so that they could be recognized.

Ann had told Bryce that Dawson had gotten life without parole. The prison would be contacted to find out who was visiting Art Dawson these days.

Bruce had a retired Marine buddy who might be interested in working routine security for Peterson Enterprise until this crisis was addressed. The whole idea of others being put in danger because of her upset Ann, but she trusted Bryce. She knew he was willing to do whatever it took to keep her safe. Bruce and Luke were the experts. Bryce and the rest of the family would defer to their judgment.

Chapter 48

The first call went to the Hudson County Police Academy. They did indeed have a dog Luke could buy. They had found him in Germany, had made a rather hefty deposit toward the purchase price, and then lost the funding. The balance was due on receipt of a healthy dog and "Gunner" was already en route.

The police department provided Bruce with all the records they had on the two convicted officers. Thompson had served his time and was released. He was married and worked in a factory, making middle-class money. He had a couple of kids.

From what Bruce could find out, he was a family man who probably wouldn't risk losing what he had to get revenge on Ann for something that happened long ago. His record had been clean since, so he wasn't considered a serious threat. But anything was possible. They had his address. Luke would check him out.

Art Dawson, it seemed, had been raped with a broom handle and stabbed to death in prison. One less worry, as far as Luke was concerned.

Not much information could be found on Maynard Lewis. According to Bobby, he had effectively dropped off the radar. It was a loose end. Bobby was concerned.

Luke and Bruce relayed all of this carefully gathered information to the rest of the family the next day.

"Now let's brainstorm and devise a plan to keep everyone safe," an uncharacteristically serious Georgio began. "All comments and suggestions will be considered."

"Maybe it would be worth our time to find Lewis's wife, Harriet. It's possible after he lost all his money that he went back to her. At least he would have a roof over his head. From what you have told us, Mom, she loved him enough to forgive all his short comings and take him back," Bobby suggested.

Ann's heart jumped into her throat. Could they find her beloved Harriet? Bryce knew immediately what Ann was thinking.

"I agree. We should find her and have a chat. It's also absolutely essential that this information be kept in the family. I don't want the media to get even a whiff of this. Ann's life could depend on how we handle everything. Does everyone understand how serious this is? Can I count on all of you?" Bryce quietly asked.

One could always count on Bobby to come up with something profound during a crisis.

"Well...we'll fight if we have to," he said with great bravado. "We aren't going to let anything happen to Mom," to which the other "kids" loudly agreed.

They discussed every possible scenario and options for containment. They all agreed the restaurant would remain open and the team would dance. All the necessary precautions would be taken, but they refused to huddle in a corner and wait for something that might never happen.

Fred Bigilow, "Biggy" for short, would be arriving on Friday. Bruce had called him about a security gig. He was getting tired of retirement anyway and was up for a challenge. For now, he would take one of the extra rooms across from the security office at Vincenzo's.

Wednesday night the restaurant opened as usual and the evening went off without a hitch. As soon as Ann and Bryce arrived they were inundated with people wanting autographs and pictures. It had been decided before hand that either Bruce or Luke would remain nearby. If people pressed too close, one of them would step in.

Asia had finally agreed to sit with the family at their table when the restaurant was open.

"If Ann can be brave, so can Asia," she said when asked what prompted this decision.

Butch was now free to become a permanent fixture by the door. Some of the guests thought it odd. If they asked, they were told it was just part of the routine security at Vincenzo's where everyone's safety was important.

The off-duty police officers who worked part-time manning the parking lot when the restaurant was open were given pictures of Thompson and Lewis. If anyone saw either man, they were to alert Bruce or Luke immediately.

Chapter 49

Biggy was a man in his forties who had kept his military attitude and haircut. He approached Bruce and Luke in size, having spent considerable time in the gym upon discharge from the Marine Corp.

He had been married four times and considered himself to be quite the ladies' man. Bruce laid out for him, in no uncertain terms, that the "Peterson women" were all off limits. He understood completely, but it didn't stop him from flirting outrageously.

He was not your run-of-the-mill, regular security kind of guy. He wouldn't be wearing a tuxedo and walking among the guests during dinner. He would be working behind the scenes, in dark corners and in obscure places. He assured the family that they would hardly ever see him.

He wore fatigues and dark paint under his eyes, which seemed like overkill to Bryce, but Bruce had confidence in the man so everyone accepted him "as is." He had his own firepower and was an expert marksman. Bobby called him "Rambo," but not to his face.

Being extremely thorough and taking his job seriously, Biggy had done his own research on the men in question. He needed to know every little thing about them. He had known a thousand maggots like these two.

They probably didn't have the guts to do their own dirty work. Most likely they would send other little worms to wreak havoc. He would be watching for them as well. He had worked with dogs during his military service so it was all good as far as he was concerned.

Gunner would be available sometime next week. He would be trained primarily to protect Ann. Butch would remain with Asia or at the restaurant door.

Where Bruce had gotten the beat up old Chevy on such short notice, no one could imagine. He said he needed a non-descript car for surveillance and he would be following Ann and Bryce home at night, making sure they were inside and buttoned up before he left.

Once they were inside with the security systems activated, they would be relatively safe. He would also be making drive-by's of the estate at random hours.

The "Peterson Clan" was now a force to be reckoned with. They would protect each other and stand together no matter what. Anyone who tried to hurt Ann, or any other member of the family, had better bring their "A-game."

Chapter 50

When they were alone, Bryce held Ann close as they sat together in the recliner by the window. From this vantage point, they had a panoramic view of their back "yard," stretching all the way to the woods beyond.

Their closeness had a calming effect on them both. When Ann lifted her face to his, Bryce knew that she had found an inner peace. They would handle this just like they handled everything. Together.

Tuesday morning Gunner arrived. He was a beautiful German Shepherd, in excellent condition. He had been trained to defend against, and/or subdue, any assailant on commend or when he sensed a threat to those he was responsible for protecting. Everyone was a little bit scared of him, if truth be known. Biggy and Bruce seemed to handle him without any concern.

There was something bothering Ann. She needed to talk to Bruce. He wanted to bring Gunner by anyway so Ann suggested he come early for dinner. The house smelled delicious when he arrived.

"Pork roast, right?" Bruce commented as he sniffed the air appreciatively. He commanded Gunner to stay by the door as he came in and washed his hands at the kitchen sink.

Ann grinned at Bryce. She was happy Bruce finally felt at home with them. After they had eaten, Bruce helped pick up the table, telling Ann what a mean pork roast she cooked. He also appreciated the brownies and coffee that followed in the living room.

Finally the conversation got around to what was on Ann's mind. She squeezed Bruce's hand.

"I'm so thankful for everything you are doing for me, Bruce. There is just one thing I need you to know that maybe you haven't thought about. I know Gunner is supposed to be protecting me, but if anyone watched Bryce and me together, they would soon learn that the way to hurt me would be to go after him."

Her eyes filled with tears as she hid her face in her husband's shoulder. His arms went around her. The need to protect Ann at all costs was his only thought. That someone might come after him to hurt her had never occurred to him. She was right. It had not escaped Bruce, however. He had already planned on working the dog with both of them and had alerted Biggy.

Ann was very relieved. If something happened to Bryce...well, she couldn't live without him. She wouldn't even try. She knew he felt the same way about her.

They had a symbiotic relationship that was extremely rare. Bruce recognized it for what it was. He sincerely wished he could find the same thing for himself. He was a big, tough guy with a marshmallow for a heart. Ann had known that from the start.

The dog was huge. He scared Ann to death. As she peeked out from behind Bryce, he whined and cocked his head to the side.

Bryce laughed. "I think he's already crazy about you, sweetie."

Ann slowly extended her hand to Gunner, hoping it came back with all fingers intact. He sniffed, licked and gave her his paw. She dropped to her knees, and hugging the big dog around his neck, she buried her face in his thick fur.

From that moment on, Gunner was devoted to Ann and he went with her and Bryce everywhere. The good citizens of Cedarville would just have to get used to it. His collar contained a special transmitter. If Bryce activated a button on his wristwatch, Bruce, Luke and Biggy could listen to what was going on around Gunner as well as give him commands.

Biggy had come up with this little device. They had tried it in the field. It worked perfectly. Not only could they find the dog no matter where he was, they could also direct him if necessary. It took a little while for Gunner to respond to a voice coming from his collar, but he was smart. He caught on.

Chapter 51

D anielle Sullivan and The Channel Nine News team were very persistent. They would not take "No" for an answer. The security was in place, so the family finally decided to do the interview. It took place one night, right before the restaurant opened for the evening festivities.

Danielle and her camera crew were invited to stay for dinner and dancing as guests of the house. Bryce and Ann, John and Carla, Georgio and Rosa were seated on the couch in front of the fireplace with the kids seated on stools behind the couch. Bruce and Luke occupied chairs at each end. Butch sat beside Luke's chair. Gunner lay at Ann's feet.

Danielle was a bit intimidated by the presence of two big dogs, prompting her first question.

"Why the dogs?"

Luke was prepared to answer.

"Peterson Enterprise has far outgrown anything we ever anticipated. We never thought the dance team would be so popular. Mama's lasagna seems to be what everyone wants to eat...we needed to increase security and do it quickly. The dogs are just an extension of that. They are both very good-natured dogs, but they are especially trained to act on command."

"They won't eat me, will they?" Danielle asked, still skeptical.

"Not unless I tell them to," Luke chuckled.

The rest of the interview went well. No questions were asked that put anyone at risk. Georgio got to talk about his glory days in European dance competition and how it compared to today in America. Of course, Ann and Bryce were asked what they had that made them so special. The answer was a simple one.

"We just love each other," Bryce said as he kissed Ann's hand and smiled into her eyes.

Biggy was the only one not present or mentioned. He was their secret weapon.

After the interview aired, it became almost impossible to get a reservation for dinner at Vincenzo's. Dancing, without dinner, remained open to all for a nominal cover charge. It was standing room only just for the dancing! Almost every night Vincenzo's was open, it was filled to capacity.

Gunner had his place at the edge of the raised band platform, giving him a view of the entire room. Butch sat at the door. Everyone got use to seeing them.

Chapter 52

During the break between sets one evening, while the band took fifteen, members of the dance team mingled with the guests, posing for pictures and signing autographs. This evening was no different from any other.

Bryce and Ann were chatting with a couple who had driven in from a neighboring state when out of nowhere Bryce heard a familiar voice.

"Well, look who it is."

Bryce recognized the nasal twang and the sarcastic attitude instantly. He excused himself and Ann from the surprised couple and turned to Victoria Templeton and Julia Prentice. Monica's two best friends.

"Tory" and "Jules" had helped Monica snare Bryce. They held nothing but contempt for him. After Monica's death they had quickly turned to other pastimes and friends. They completely forgot about Bryce, unconcerned about the havoc they had helped cause in his life. Not being interested in dancing, they didn't follow the competitions. Neither of them ever even watched the news unless they were mentioned in it.

Tory had heard a business associate of her husband's rave about some place in Cedarville, north of Dixon, called Vincenzo's. He had gone on and on about how great the food was, what a wonderful band they had and actually compared it to Andre's, for heaven's sake. Andre's was considered to be the hottest spot in the area!

Tory decided she and Jules were going to go check it out. She badgered her husband until he called for reservations. It took several months before a table was open. She was furious. After all, she was Victoria Templeton. Couldn't he pull some strings or something? Apparently not. She would just have to wait.

They arrived for dinner on a Friday evening several months later and were shown immediately to their table. When they went to the powder room to freshen up, Tory had to admit to Jules that the place really was beautiful. On their way back to the table Tory stopped short.

"Look over there," she hissed, tipping her head toward the spot where Ann and Bryce stood. "Let's go poke the little toad with a stick."

As they turned toward the approaching women, Ann felt Bryce tense as beads of perspiration popped out on his upper lip, something she hadn't seen in a long time. He drew her close.

"Can I help you ladies in some way?" Bryce, always the gentleman, asked the two vipers.

Since it was a Friday night, all the dancers were in "full dress." Ann and Bryce were both wearing white. Bryce looked exceedingly handsome to Ann in his white cutaway tuxedo. She was wearing a floor length sequined white gown, off the right shoulder and slit to just above her left knee. Her hair was held in place on top of her head by a small white comb sparkling with diamonds.

The fact that Ann and Bryce made a striking couple was not lost on Victoria. Bryce had never been anything but courteous to her, no matter how rudely she treated him. That chivalrous attitude of his made her hate him for no other reason than that she had never been able to bring him down to her level.

"You never did know how to dress yourself did you, Bryce? Isn't that get-up a little too much?" Tory snorted rudely. "I see you're still a bald, little, pathetic worm of a man."

She turned to Ann, looking her up and down.

"Oh and isn't this nice, you've found someone just your size. How pitiful."

Shock registered on Ann's face. Her hand went to Bryce's chest where his hand at once covered hers. Neither noticed Gunner quietly trot up and stand at Ann's knee until they heard the deep rumble coming from his throat.

Tory was too stupid to be paying attention. She was too caught up in humiliating Bryce.

"And where is that little moron who followed you around everywhere?"

Luke had seen Gunner move, saw the stricken look on his mother's face and had stepped up behind the two women just in time to hear Tory's last comment.

"That little moron is right here," he said quietly.

Tory jumped and spun around. She had to look up...way up... to see the young man standing over her with a pleasant smile on his face, belying the hard look in his eyes.

Gunner's hair was standing up on his back, the growl beginning to roll unabated, as he took a position between Ann and the now terrified women who had at least enough sense not to move. The dog meant business.

"I want the police called right now! This dog is going to attack us."

Luke flipped open his badge and stuck it in Victoria's face.

"Scary isn't it?" he said with sarcasm that Ann had never heard coming from this mild-mannered young man.

"Then I demand to speak to the owner of this establishment."

As Bryce looked into the face of his beautiful wife, who trusted him completely, he regained his composure.

"I AM the owner of this establishment."

Suddenly, nothing Victoria or Julia could say had the power to make him feel small any more.

Bruce, looking splendid in his black tuxedo, had seen what was happening and stepped up beside Ann.

"Ladies, if you can behave yourselves you are welcome to go back to your table and enjoy the rest of the evening. If you are unable to accomplish that small task, you will be escorted to your car."

No one had ever spoken to Tory in that manner before in her life. For the first time, she was definitely NOT in control and she didn't like it.

"Come on Tory, I want to stay. Let's go back to the table," pleaded a contrite Julia.

Tory glared at Bryce. "Fine," she said as she whipped around, almost stepping into Luke.

Luke gallantly bowed at the waist holding out his hand to the two embarrassed women.

"Ladies, this way please," he said as he directed them back to their smirking husbands.

"Wow. Wish I had that on tape," said an astounded Randolph Templeton.

"It was worth a month's salary just to witness it," agreed an equally amused Troy Prentice.

Chapter 53

Fortunately, not many people had observed this little altercation. Bruce and Luke were very pleased with the way Gunner had behaved. If a dog could look self-satisfied, that's how Gunner looked as he returned to his place on the platform.

Back at the family table, Ann hugged Bryce tight. She loved him so much.

"Honey, I'm so proud of you," she whispered against his ear.

His heart flipped over the way it always did when she looked at him like that; her eyes shining, her lips curved in a smile, her dimples dancing. He felt ten feet tall. He wished they could go home right now!

It had become their practice to spot-light one of the couples every night at the beginning of open dancing. Tonight it was Ann and Bryce.

"Ladies and gentleman. Welcome to the Vincenzo Ballroom. I'm Luke Peterson."

Luke had become a favorite with the patrons who frequented Vincenzo's, as well as with people on the dance circuit. He received thunderous applause, which he accepted graciously, with a crooked grin.

"Please show your appreciation for our talented band, led by Jimmy O'Brien."

He waited for the applause to die down.

"And how was everyone's dinner? Everybody have enough?"

More applause, this time with whistles and shouting.

"Thanks to our wonderful chef, as well as the kitchen and wait staff," Luke continued as the staff took positions behind the buffet table. "If you have been our guest before, you know Gunner and Butch."

Both dogs gave a sharp, short bark.

"Although they are friendly, please don't pet them, they're working dogs. And finally, for your enjoyment, in tonight's spotlight dance, may I present Bryce and Lauren Ann Peterson, my Mom and Dad."

Everyone stood and began clapping. In order to see what was going on Victoria and Julia were forced to stand, which galled Tory to no end. As the intro to the music started, the audience sat down and the dance began. How they felt about each other was obvious. They danced like no one was watching.

"How beautiful," Julia breathed. "I've heard they're called The King and Queen of Romance. I can understand why!"

"Oh, puh-lease," Tory responded, painfully drawing out the word with a roll of her eyes.

She never knew Bryce could dance like that! Monica had always said he was a clumsy oaf. Maybe she had lied about other things too. Their dancing was certainly mesmerizing.

Around midnight, Bryce and Ann, accompanied by Gunner, quietly took their leave. The younger folks would stay until the bitter end to clean up and close up.

No one paid any attention to the well dressed gentleman standing at the back when he left just seconds behind the Petersons. He had come early and parked his car where he could leave without undue attention. He pulled out a couple of car lengths behind Ann and Bryce, following them at a distance.

Chapter 54

Tony Marco decided to do some checking on his own. The Petersons lived on a gated estate and owned a manufacturing company and the restaurant. They had every security precaution known to the free world and Ann Peterson was surrounded by people who loved her.

Loyalty was something his uncle, crime boss Dominic Marco, expected above all else. Tony felt he had proven himself over and over again. Since age fourteen, he had been running errands and doing odd jobs for his uncle. He was tired of it. Now was his chance to move up in the organization.

He decided it would behoove him to put some effort into good surveillance with accurate details; show his uncle he had initiative. A plan of action began taking shape in his mind as he followed the white Mercedes.

When Bryce slowed down to make the turn into the driveway, Tony was close enough to read the license plate number. As he watched the back of the car wind up the driveway to the house, he saw Gunner's face staring at him out the rear window.

Hummm, he thought to himself. *I'll have to come up with some way to eliminate the damn dog!*

Tony continued up the road until he came to the end of the Peterson Estate where the security fence turned right into the woods. The Peterson's property apparently abutted a National Park and there was a utility road running parallel to their fence. It looked unused as weeds and small bushes had grown up in the tire tracks.

Not wanting to get his only good suit dirty, Tony decided the best course of action would be to come back during the day and check out this road. Maybe he could find a vantage point where he could remain hidden and still spy on the house and grounds. He would have to remember to bring his high-powered binoculars.

Chapter 55

O nce inside, Bryce tossed his keys into the decorative box that sat on the wooden cabinet across from the coat closet. Taking his wife in his arms, he kissed her soundly.

"Welcome home, sweetheart," he whispered in her ear. "Thank you for a wonderful evening."

This had become their routine ever since they had moved into this house. They were always so glad to be home, finally alone.

Gunner lapped up the water left in his bowl from earlier in the day and headed toward the sliding glass doors leading out onto the patio. The transmitter on his collar opened and closed the door, allowing him to come and go as needed.

He would not only be taking care of his own personal nightly business, he would also be checking the perimeter of the house and immediate grounds, as he had been taught to do, every time he went out.

Bryce fixed Ann and himself a cup of tea. Ann brought out a plate of cookies. A little bedtime snack was in order.

Ann had a mischievous twinkle in her eyes.

"We'll need the energy for the rest of the night's activities."

Finally, safe and sound in their king-sized bed, their lovemaking was all-consuming. Tomorrow would be another busy day. Thankfully, measures were in place to protect them both. They drifted peacefully off to sleep to the strains of Kenny G's saxophone.

Gunner dropped his head to his paws as he curled up on the rug in front of the fireplace in the living room. From this spot, he could see the front and back doors as well as the door to the patio. This was the perfect spot from which to guard his new family.

Chapter 56

A week later, careful not to disturb the weeds and bushes in the middle of the utility road, Tony made his way along the Peterson fence. He had left his car in the park's parking lot so that he could go on foot into the woods. No one would be suspicious of a young guy with a backpack wearing hiking boots.

He had walked about a mile along the road when the Peterson fence ended. *What a lucky break*, he thought. He sat his pack down and pulled out a water bottle. Anyone just looking from the road would assume the fence went all the way around the property. Finishing the water and a bag of chips he began scouting the area for a nice tall, sturdy tree.

Finding exactly what he wanted about a hundred yards on up the road, he climbed as high as he could. Wedging himself between the trunk and a large branch, he got out his binoculars and began scanning the area all the way to the house.

Tony had convinced his uncle that he was ready for bigger and better things than picking up pay-offs and delivering "product." The Peterson's were worth millions and Dominic Marco had it on good authority that the husband would pay any price to protect his wife.

"We're going to snatch the beautiful Mrs. Peterson and ask for ten million dollars ransom," Dominic told his nephew. "Then I'm going to have Big Sal snuff the guy who is asking for my help with this job. I'll keep all the money and do what I want with the woman."

Laughing so hard he choked, Dominic continued.

"Don't fail me and you will become my right hand man. Maybe even take over the business someday. I ain't as young as I used to be."

With this promise bouncing around in his head, Tony paid close attention to what was happening across the lake. He had some ideas of his own he would present to his uncle when the time was right.

The security cameras were at each corner of the house and were, most likely, motion sensitive. He guessed lights came on at dusk and went off at dawn. No trees or shrubs were close enough to the house to provide good cover. Tony scrambled down the tree. *Man! This won't be easy. I won't be able to snatch her from the house. I'll have to figure out some other way...*

Over the ensuing week, Tony climbed to his perch at different times during the day and into the evening, watching carefully so as not to miss anything. So far, he hadn't seen anything useful.

On Monday nights, the restaurant was closed so Tony decided he would spend the late afternoon and evening watching the house. He took snacks and water up the tree with him and settled in for the long haul.

He couldn't see in through the windows, thanks to the one-way glass. *The lights must stay on all the time because everything looks exactly the same during the day as it does right now,* he thought at around eight-thirty that evening.

He was about ready to call it a night when the door to the patio opened just wide enough for the dog to go out, immediately closing after him. *Must be going out for his last pee of the night,* Tony mused. *Guess I'd better head back and get some sleep. Everything looks closed down for the night. I'll check in with Uncle Dom in the morning.*

Tony was too busy getting himself and his knapsack down the tree to notice that the dog had gone trotting off, his nose to the ground. As he was about to drop from the last branch to the ground, he heard a formidable sound. He looked down into the glowing eyes and bared teeth of one huge German Shepherd.

OH, SHIT, he cursed as he was scrambling back up the tree. *What the hell am I going to do now?*

To his relief, a man stepped out onto the patio and whistled. The dog responded immediately, but not before giving Tony one last long look. It made his blood run cold. He hated dogs. Especially this one.

Chapter 57

Bryce had decided he wanted some buttermilk and toast before going to bed so Ann was busy at the kitchen counter. Bryce sat on a stool at the island bar watching her.

He loved sitting on this stool. Sitting down brought his face to the exact level of Ann's. She would stand between his knees, her arms around his neck with her lips brushing his cheek. He would hold her close breathing in the delicate perfume she wore especially because he liked it. They sometimes had long intimate talks about any number of things in this very spot.

Tonight Ann buried her face in his shoulder. She was subdued, which was unlike her.

"Honey, what's wrong?" Bryce said as he gently pulled her back and looked into her face.

"The other night at the ballroom. That awful woman! She said such terrible things to you, Bryce! And she called Luke a MORON! I wanted to scratch her eyes out!"

Angry tears ran unchecked down her cheeks.

Bryce had wondered when Ann would get around to discussing what had happened at the ballroom with Victoria and Julia.

"I know," Bryce sighed. "I feel sorry for their husbands."

Ann giggled despite her dismay. He always knew exactly what to say to make her feel better.

They finished their snack and Bryce went to the door and whistled for the dog.

"I wonder what Gunner's up to out here. He usually doesn't take this long."

Gunner came promptly, but didn't curl up in his usual spot. Rather he paced from the patio door to the front door and back several times. Bryce checked the cameras and the alarm system. Everything was working properly. Bryce called Bruce...just in case.

Meanwhile, out in the woods, Tony hugged the tree until he stopped shaking. He finally slid down the trunk and headed for his car.

H O L Y C R A P! That was a close one!

Bruce arrived in ten minutes. He took a quick look at the surveillance camera pictures. Nothing. Door locks were all functional. Everything was as it should be. He signaled Gunner and they headed out the door.

They started at the front gate and began working their way around the perimeter of the property. Gunner immediately headed in the direction of the woods. Bruce had learned to trust the dog's leading and followed at a fast trot. It didn't take any time at all before he was barking at the tree where Tony had been only an hour ago.

Bruce bagged a couple of cigarette butts and some candy wrappers. With any luck DNA would be lurking in the saliva. It was obvious someone had been up the tree.

He climbed gingerly from branch to branch until he found a spot with a perfect view of the front of the house and down two sides. Whoever had been up here could see the patio door and the garage door at side angles with a full on view of the front door while remaining out of camera range. Clever. This person must have had some knowledge of the estate. The cameras were well hidden, yet no pictures were captured.

A couple pieces of fabric were caught on one of the twigs. They were carefully collected and put into a separate evidence bag. At daylight, Bruce would have a crime scene team up here to go over every inch of the tree and surrounding ground all the way to the road. The Park Service would also be notified. Maybe someone had seen something.

There was a nice big bone waiting for Gunner upon his return to the house. He had done exactly what he had been trained to do. Bruce was very pleased. He explained the evidence he had collected to Ann and Bryce telling them to expect a forensics team to be swarming all over the place at first light.

He and Gunner took one last look around. Whoever the peeping Tom was, he was gone now. Gunner finished his bone, circled a couple of times and laid down. All was well for the time being. Bruce left to bring Luke and Biggy up to speed on the latest developments. Maybe Biggy had seen something that would make sense when added to what Bruce now knew.

Biggy did indeed have some observations. Several nights ago, he had spotted a car parked along the side of the road just up from the restaurant instead of in the parking lot. When he had run the plates they came up as stolen. No surprise there. The police had been alerted at the time and an APB was put out on the plate number. If this guy was smart, he would ditch the car. *That's what I would do,* Biggy thought.

A week later, they found the car abandoned behind the local Wal-Mart. It was wiped clean of prints and had been vacuumed. It was spotless.

Biggy's gut told him this was their guy.

"Damn," he shouted as he pounded his fist on the roof of the car. "We lost him."

Chapter 58

Ann was surprisingly calm considering the activity of the last couple of days. Bryce was the anxious one. He loved her so much! He couldn't imagine how he would survive if something happened to her. She looked at him with such trust in her eyes. He only hoped he could live up to her expectations.

Bryce had been planning a little surprise for Ann. He decided now was a good time to make it happen. They could both use a few days away from the stress of the current situation.

"Pack some clothes, sweetheart. We're going on a little trip. And, no, I won't give you any details because it's a surprise," Bryce told her. "Take some evening wear as well as casual clothes and comfortable shoes."

Ann hugged him tight.

"Why all the secrecy?"

"You'll see, my love. You'll see," was the mysterious reply.

The drive to the airport in Dixon was a pleasant one. The farther they got from home, the more relaxed they both felt. Gunner was riding in the back seat, looking out the window. He looked very official, wearing his K-9 vest and service dog tag.

Luke had gotten Gunner certified as a service dog, which meant he could accompany Ann and Bryce anywhere they went, including on the plane. Bryce didn't quibble about paying for an extra first class seat for the big dog. Ann didn't think it was necessary for

Gunner to go along, but Luke and Bruce insisted. Better to be prepared...just in case.

When the plane landed in Boston, Ann was apprehensive. After all, this is where it all happened. Her abuse, the trial, the threats. Gunner whined and cocked his head to the side, giving Ann a pensive look. She scratched behind his ears.

"It's okay, boy. I know you'll watch out for me."

She looked up at Bryce.

"Why are we here?"

"Just be patient," he answered with a sparkle in his eyes.

They took a cab from the airport to the hotel. Luke had made arrangements in advance, explaining the need for the dog. The manager wasn't keen on the idea, but...money talks.

It didn't take long to unpack. Meanwhile, Gunner made a thorough inspection of all the rooms and closets. He trotted back to Ann looking satisfied. After a bite to eat in the hotel restaurant, they headed down town.

Ann was still in the dark as to what her surprise was as they stood in the lobby of a huge office building. Bryce was looking intently at the list of people with offices in this particular building.

And there it was! She finally saw it. Bryce thought she would never look up. The name seemed to leap off the wall. Ann's knees went weak. Tears began to run down her face as she grabbed Bryce's arm.

Chapter 59

Gladys Avery had been the secretary in this office since before Dr. Mark Goodwin had bought the practice. She was past retirement age and she dearly wanted to move south where the climate was kinder during the winter. Her daughter and grandchildren would be close by, making it all the more desirable.

She had been a widow for several years and she was tired, just plain tired, of working. But Dr. Goodwin just wasn't an organized man and he needed her. As far as Gladys knew, he had never been married and no family ever visited.

He was prone to periods of despondency, bordering on depression, which seemed to be more and more pronounced as he got older. The smell of alcohol was sometimes on his breath and that worried Gladys. She really didn't know what to do to help him because she didn't know what the problem was...exactly.

He was a fine-looking man, tall and broad-shouldered. His salt and pepper hair was still thick and there were only a few tell-tale lines around his eyes and mouth.

He was meticulous about his appearance and was always a gentleman. He had money, charm...for the life of her, Gladys couldn't understand why some nice woman hadn't snatched him up! She knew he dated once in a while, but nothing ever developed.

She sighed and turned to her work just as the door to the waiting room opened and a nice-looking couple entered and walked up to her desk. She put on a smile and greeted them.

This must be the 11 o'clock appointment, she thought to herself. The first thing she saw was the dog. She did her best not to look as shocked by the monstrous beast as she felt. *Act natural, Gladys, like you see this every day.*

Then her eyes went to the couple standing before her. The woman was stunning. She had on a pink cashmere sweater dress and matching high heels. Her hair was attractively styled and hung past her shoulders. Her dark blue eyes were a little uncertain as she looked from her husband to Gladys.

He was much taller than she and he was bald. His gray suit and tie complemented her attire perfectly. He had a confident air about him, while still being extremely courteous and soft spoken.

This must be Mr. and Mrs. Peterson. When the appointment was made it was not for health reasons, but for personal reasons. Gladys was extremely curious. *What can this be about?*

She asked them to be seated and noticed how solicitous the man was of his wife, seating her first and then dropping his hand over hers as he sat down close beside her.

The way Mrs. Peterson looked at her husband and the interaction between the two of them reminded Gladys of how Mr. Avery had looked at her when they were young. She didn't have time to think about all this right now. Later tonight, with a cup of hot tea, the whole situation would require some thought.

Dr. Goodwin answered his phone on the first ring. Gladys informed him that the Petersons were waiting. A scowl crossed her face as he said he really couldn't see them now, he needed to go home.

"Be a doll, Gladys. Get them to reschedule."

She hung up the phone and beckoned them forward.

"Something has come up," she told them. "You will have to make another appointment."

Chapter 60

With one look, Bryce knew how disappointed Ann was. In a flash, Gladys realized how important this visit must be to them.

"Could I have a small piece of paper and an envelope?" Bryce asked patiently. "When he reads this, if he still cannot see us, we understand and we will leave."

He quickly wrote on the paper, sealed it in the envelope and asked that Gladys give this message to the doctor.

Gladys took the note and hurried down the hall to Dr. Goodwin's private office. *This is getting better and better.*

When she entered, Dr. Goodwin was bent over his desk with his head in his hands.

Gladys switched into her "mother mode" and said, "Mark, I think you need to see these people."

He looked up in surprise. She had never questioned his decisions before.

She handed him the envelope.

Reluctantly, he took it.

"What's this?" he asked.

"I suggest you open it and see."

He opened it slowly. As soon as his eyes rested on what was written, he jumped up so fast his chair flew backwards, crashing into the bookcase behind his desk. He ran around the corner of his desk almost knocking Gladys over in the process.

She regained her footing and followed him out into the hall. She watched him pause before he opened the door to the waiting room. He smoothed back his hair and took a couple of deep breaths.

He opened the door and stared in disbelief at the woman sitting in his waiting room. The envelope and paper fluttered to the floor, forgotten. Gladys picked it up. Only a name was written on it. Kathy Martin.

His mouth formed one word, "Kathy?"

She walked to him and took both his hands in hers. His eyes searched her face.

"Yes," she said, "It's Kathy. My name is Lauren Ann Peterson now and this is my husband, Bryce. Everyone calls me Ann."

Bryce came forward, his arm encircling her waist.

Memories came flooding over Mark. He thought he would never see her again; not after the US Marshall took her away. An emergency at the hospital had kept him from saying goodbye. He had known it was for her safety and it had taken every bit of strength he had to send her away. He had missed her terribly for all these years.

He had kept an image of her in his mind and heart and now, here she was. He must be imagining it. How could she be here? He just stood there holding her hands, unable to do more.

Gladys, being a very perceptive woman, stood by and watched with interest as this little scenario played out right before her eyes. *So this is why Dr. Goodwin has never married and why he has become more and more forlorn as the years go by. He has been missing someone all this time!*

Bryce gave her a nod and a smile of gratitude. She took this as her cue to be on her way. She would probably never know what this was all about or who Kathy Martin, aka Mrs. Peterson was, but something told her that retirement might not be so far off after all! She left with a smile and a backward glance at Dr. Goodwin, who still had not managed to say another word.

"Ka... I mean Ann," he finally croaked. "What are you doing here?"

"I never got to thank you for everything you did for me; for saving my life and being my friend," Ann said. "They took me west immediately after the trial and they wouldn't let me see you or call you. Before we were married, I told Bryce everything. He knows how much this has bothered me. He found you for me and made this appointment. Thanks for seeing us," she said with a quirky grin.

The dam that had held back his emotions for so long finally broke and he squeezed Ann to his chest. Sobs erupted from deep down. Tears flowed with abandon. Finally drained, he thrust her back, staring into her face.

"You're all right." It was a statement not so much a question. "You're all grown up and beautiful," he gulped. "And you're happy!"

This realization became too much for the big man. He turned and dropped into one of the waiting room chairs. Bryce pulled two other chairs close to his and as Mark re-grouped, Bryce and Ann explained how they came to be sitting in his office and why a police dog accompanied them everywhere they went.

Mark hadn't even noticed Gunner until then. The expression on his face changed from disbelief, to wonderment and then to joy.

"Have you guys eaten yet?" he asked. "Because I'm suddenly starving."

They went to a quaint little restaurant a couple of blocks from Mark's office building. Gunner laid down under the table at Ann's feet. Everyone stared, but they were not questioned as to the presence of the dog. As they lingered over coffee, Ann updated Mark on everything that had transpired after she was relocated and given a new identity.

Bryce marveled at how calmly she talked about her life alone in a strange city, her fears and struggles and eventually her successes. Mark interjected a question now and then, his eyes never leaving her face as he paid close attention to everything she said. He was like a thirsty man getting his first drink of water.

She was the most courageous person Bryce had ever known. He was so proud of her. He liked the animated way her expressions changed as she filled Mark in on the past eighteen to twenty years of her life.

Let's face it, Bryce admitted to himself. *I'm the luckiest man alive and I just love looking at her!*

Chapter 61

As they were getting ready to leave, Bryce said he was taking Ann to an exclusive club called "Up Town" that evening for dinner and dancing.

"We would love to have you join us," he said to Mark. "That is, if you don't already have other plans."

Mark accepted on one condition. They had to spend the whole weekend in Boston and since he had a guest room in his townhouse, they had to stay with him. He had a surprise of his own for Ann and he could hardly wait to show her. It was something he never thought she would see.

Since dinner wouldn't be until seven-thirty, they had plenty of time to pack their things, pay their bill at the hotel and be ready for Mark to pick them up in about an hour. He was right on time.

His townhouse was in a quiet, respectable neighborhood and he did indeed have a large guest room on the second floor, all prepared for them. His tastes were simple and masculine, but comfortable. In the living room were a large sofa, loveseat and recliner grouped together around a beautiful oriental rug with floor lamps giving off a soft glow.

In the center was a well-used coffee table where Ann noticed medical journals, today's newspaper, a notepad and pen, not to mention a coffee cup from that morning. The entertainment center held a big screen TV and a stereo system.

The good-sized kitchen with an oak table and four chairs was off to the right and was immaculate. *He must have a housekeeper,* Ann decided. *A bachelor couldn't possibly be this neat.*

The sofa pillows, draperies and curtains were coordinated to match the furniture giving the place a homey feel. There was only one thing missing; a woman's touch.

Ann and Bryce got situated in their room and since Mark had some paperwork to finish on one of his patients, they decided to take a nap. It would undoubtedly be a late night. Gunner curled up on the floor beside the bed.

Chapter 62

A round five o'clock they hopped into the shower and began to get ready for their evening out. This club required formal wear and they had come prepared with the right clothes for the occasion.

Bryce looked extremely handsome to Ann in his black tuxedo. He was always neat, clean shaven and smelled good without being overpowering. Bryce could see the approval in her eyes and he grinned at her.

She was wearing a sapphire blue gown. The dress was slightly flared from the hips and hung to her ankles; the perfect length for dancing. Her hair was held in place on top of her head by a jeweled comb, which was the only accessory she wore besides pierced single diamond stud earrings.

She carried a small matching clutch bag, which contained her lip gloss, a comb, driver's license and twenty dollars...just in case. In fact, it was the exact same twenty dollars Harriet had given her all those years ago. She kept it in memory of her lost friend.

Simple but elegant. It suits her perfectly, Bryce thought as he pulled her to him for a kiss.

"Have I told you lately how much I love you," he whispered into her ear.

Gunner wore his usual.

They had waited only a short time in the living room before Mark came down the stairs. He was also dressed in a tuxedo and looked...amazing. Ann knew there would be no shortage of partners for the good doctor this evening.

Bryce had reserved a table by the window and they were seated immediately. The maitre d' looked askance at the dog, but said nothing. The menu was in French, which, as luck would have it, Ann could read and speak fluently. She had a gift for languages and had studied several during her college years.

She translated for the two men and a very efficient waiter took their orders. Their drinks arrived, ice water with lemon for Ann and Bryce and a double scotch on the rocks for Mark. This surprised Ann since as a young man, he never drank. She would tuck this observation away and be watchful.

The conversation ebbed and flowed as the men enjoyed their steaks and Ann her salmon. Mark casually ordered another double scotch. Bryce and Ann exchanged looks. When the dishes had been cleared away and the coffee was served, the orchestra gathered and the music began.

They watched the dance floor fill with other guests. Then Bryce took Ann's hand and in one smooth motion, helped her to her feet. He guided her to an empty spot and they joined the other couples circling the floor.

Several women gave Mark an admiring stare, but he didn't seem to notice. Instead, he nursed his drink and watched. It was bittersweet for him. He had known from the start he was too old for Kath... Ann. He would have married her anyway knowing she would accept, not because she was *in love* with him, but because she loved him and felt indebted to him.

He supposed her feelings for him were more in line with an older brother or uncle. He knew for sure she did care about him and she trusted him. He wanted more for her than that, so he let her go. There hadn't been a day that went by that he hadn't thought about her and wondered if she was all right.

As Mark watched them dance together, it became obvious to him how they felt about each other and how protective Bryce was of her. It helped temper the disappointment he felt. All he had ever wanted was for her to be safe and happy. So why did he suddenly feel so rotten?

He signaled the waiter to bring him another drink. It helped if the edges of his emotions were a little fuzzy. Gunner nuzzled Mark's arm and whined. Even the dog knew all was not well.

Chapter 63

During the break the conductor approached their table and introduced himself. He asked Bryce if he and Ann were the Petersons from Vincenzo's Ballroom. They were surprised that they were known this far from home.

The conductor, who said his name was Merle Jennings, had been to Vincenzo's and had seen them perform. He had been impressed and asked if they would mind taking the spotlight for one song this evening.

"I know your music and it would be an honor to play for you," he stated with a satisfied smile.

They agreed and when the second set began Merle announced that they had a treat in store for them this evening. Mr. and Mrs. Peterson from Vincenzo's Ballroom in Cedarville, Vermont had graciously agreed to dance for them. People applauded politely. Nobody knew them and this crowd was not going to be easily impressed by "out-of-towners."

The strains of *Unforgettable* began, much to Ann's delight. It was, in fact, their signature song. Bryce pulled her into his arms and they gazed at each other for only a second before they began to dance. After that, they were alone in a world all their own with only the music and the pleasure they felt dancing together.

They definitely had a quality that was new to everyone watching. Romance. Pure and simple. The way he held her close, their bodies moving effortlessly across the floor and the way they looked at each other...oh my! It was mesmerizing and mystical and wonderful.

It was apparent that they were also technically excellent as their footwork was intricate and the lifts they did were original and exciting to watch. When the song ended, Bryce swept her up in his arms and with their foreheads pressed together, he carried her slowly back to their table and gently put her down.

The onlookers stood in unison and applauded in earnest. Hand in hand they came back out on the floor and Ann dropped into a deep curtsy as Bryce bowed slightly, still holding Ann's hand. Those watching realized that they had indeed witnessed something special...and the Vincenzo Ballroom's reputation grew.

Ann and Bryce danced several times through the next two sets of music, being interrupted over and over by people wanting to express appreciation for their performance. Bryce was always humble and gracious when accepting compliments on their behalf.

Around midnight they decided to call it a night and Mark asked the maitre d' to have his car brought around. Ann and Bryce were worried as they waited for the car, each for different reasons.

Bryce wondered if Mark should be driving after having so much to drink. He was a big man and he had probably consumed that much alcohol before. Hopefully, he could drive without mishap. Bryce decided if he saw any indication that Mark could not safely drive, he would step in.

Ann, on the other hand, was extremely concerned that her "Dr. Mark" lived such a lonely existence and coped by drinking. He was so unhappy. It hurt her heart to see him like that, not to mention she worried about the risks to his health.

Chapter 64

Fortunately they made it back to the house without incident. Ann wanted to change into something more comfortable so she and Bryce headed up to their room. When they were alone they quickly discussed their concerns regarding Mark.

As they changed into sweatpants and t-shirts, Bryce explained his plan to Ann. By the time they came down stairs Mark was standing in the kitchen putting ice in a glass with an open bottle of scotch, his drink of choice, on the counter.

Ann quickly stepped up beside him and put her hand over the top of the glass. She tugged at his arm asking him to come and sit with her; she and Bryce wanted to talk to him about something.

His head dropped to his chest. He knew exactly what they wanted to discuss with him and in a way, he was glad that it would be out in the open. He couldn't remember the exact event that had triggered his drinking, it had just happened. Now...he needed it.

He would come home from his office or the hospital to this empty house and the ghosts of the past would join him for a microwave dinner. To blot out the memories that came creeping in, he would toss back a couple...or more, falling into a restless, tossing, turning state that he called sleep. The next morning, no matter his good intentions, he would do it all over again. He carried the guilt and self recriminations with him everywhere.

He followed Ann obediently to the sofa where she sat him down next to Bryce. Bryce guided her into his lap and her arm went automatically around his neck.

Mark reminded her of a dejected little boy about to be scolded for some infraction as he sat there looking down at his folded hands. Her heart went out to him. She hugged Bryce and gave him a little nod. What Mark heard next was not what he had expected to hear at all.

"Mark, Ann and I would like you to move to Cedarville and be part of our family. You could find a house or apartment in Cedarville, you could have a house built, or you could live at Vincenzo's. Cedarville has a good-sized hospital where you could easily get privileges and Ann would welcome your help in the free clinic."

"Wha . . . . what?" Mark finally whispered, looking back and forth between Ann and Bryce.

"We have a big 'family' and I know they would welcome you without reservation. What do you think?" Bryce persisted.

Mark just sat there, staring at them for several minutes. Time passed in slow motion as Mark processed this information through the cobwebs in his brain. *They are dead serious,* he thought as he continued to gape, mouth open.

Ann saw his hesitation and understood it. They had laid this on him without any warning.

"Okay, how about this?" Ann picked up where Bryce had left off. "Why don't you come for a visit over the holidays? Thanksgiving and Christmas are right around the corner. Come for a visit and see how everything feels to you. Then decide whether or not you want to make it permanent." Ann squeezed his arm. "And we will help you kick the drinking, Mark."

"I'll come and visit," Mark finally agreed. "I'm not going to make any promises..."

His voice trailed off and he looked away.

For the next hour, they slurped down the ice cream Ann found in the freezer and Mark was filled in on everyone who was part of the

Peterson family. He listened with interest, still not quite believing they really wanted to include him.

They went to bed after the dishes were done and the kitchen was cleaned up. As soon as they were alone, Ann showed Bryce just how much she loved him.

He trusted her completely. He had no reservations at all about Mark being in such close proximity. After all, if it hadn't been for Mark's intervention in Ann's life, he would still be alone and miserable. *I genuinely want to help Mark if I can,* he thought as he drifted off to sleep with Ann's head comfortably resting on his chest, his arms around her.

Sleep did not come quite so easily for Mark, even with the alcohol he had consumed. His mind went in circles. Should he go? Should he stay here? Should he go just for the holidays? Then how would he ever return to his boring, lonely life? Finally, near dawn, the answer became clear to him.

He could spend the rest of his life as he was, probably dying of liver disease, sad and alone, or he could go to Cedarville. He would be able to see Ann every day, work beside her and be a part of her life.

That's all of her he could ever have, but he decided that would be enough. His answer was clear. He would put his townhouse on the market and start making arrangements to sell his medical practice. He smiled to himself. *Gladys,* he thought, *pack your swimsuit and suntan lotion!*

Chapter 65

Around ten the next morning Ann and Bryce came downstairs to find Mark already busy in the kitchen. The coffee was made and he was mixing up a batter for French toast. The poor guy had dark circles under his eyes, but he was clear-headed and humming a Beach Boys tune as he dipped the bread in the batter.

It was going to be a full day. He had a couple of things he was anxious to show them before they flew back to Vermont on Sunday. Ann poured coffee all around and helped dish up the food. As they ate, Mark briefly explained his plan for the day; vague with the details. His only instructions to them were to dress casual and warm.

They all piled into Mark's car, appropriately dressed and headed toward the south side of Boston until they came to a small, well-maintained church sitting back from the road and surrounded by pine trees.

As they were getting out of the car, a portly gentleman came out to meet them. He shook Mark's hand warmly.

"This is Father Mike and this is his church," Mark told them as introductions were made.

Mark couldn't help but grin at the puzzled expression on Ann's face.

After pleasantries were exchanged and it was confirmed that the weather was, in fact, getting colder, Father Mike said, "I expect you know where you're going," and with a smile that included them all, he hurried back inside.

Mark must come here often, Ann thought. *He seems to be good friends with the Father.* This surprised her as she had not known him to be a religious man.

Mark led Ann and Bryce around the corner and down a path through the trees until they emerged into a small, well-tended cemetery. They made their way to a little clearing where Ann noticed yellow mums had been carefully planted.

Ann wondered what in the world they were doing here on this chilly morning. Mark had a solemn look on his face so she knew that whatever it was, it must be important.

She looked around, at first completely missing the tiny gravestone that rested among the fall flowers. When she finally noticed it, her whole body jerked in shock as she read what was written there.

Baby Lucas, Beloved by his Mother. The birth and death date were the same day.

Every bit of color drained from her face and her heart nearly exploded with emotion. She would have fallen if Bryce had not caught her. She clung to him for a long time, not able to trust her shaking legs, as the memory of that day flooded over her.

Her sweet baby had been born too early and had died in her arms. She never knew what had happened to his tiny body. "Dr. Mark" had taken him away, wrapped in a blue blanket. She never had the courage to question him about it. She had been so young and so afraid. Then everything that happened afterward…happened, and she was taken into witness protection.

She finally knelt down and ran her fingers slowly and lovingly over each letter. The men stepped back and allowed her time and space.

In those quiet moments, Bryce found enormous respect for the man standing next to him. He had his faults to be sure, but this had been a selfless act of kindness. One that, as far as Mark knew, would never be recognized, yet he came often to tend the little grave and plant the flowers.

Ann finally stood and looked at Mark.

"Mark," she said, struggling to hold back the tears that were about to spill over and run down her cheeks. "You have taken care of my baby all this time!"

In all the times she had come to the emergency room, badly bruised from a recent beating administered by her SOB husband, Mark had never seen her cry or heard her complain. She had even come with a broken arm and never whimpered as the bone was set.

Before they were married, Bryce had seen her cry only once and that had been when she told him about the son she lost.

Mark came to her, putting his hands on her shoulders.

"It's okay to cry, Peanut," he said choking back his own emotions.

Seeming to need his permission, she stepped into his embrace and buried her face in his chest. Her shoulders heaved as the sobs racked her body. Mark laid his cheek against the top of her head and murmured things that only she could hear.

Whatever he said seemed to calm her and slowly she pulled away and wiped her eyes.

"Mark, how can I ever thank you?" she whispered.

Then she looked at Bryce.

"If Mark comes to Cedarville, Lucas will be here all alone," she said as tears threatened to overflow again.

Bryce hugged her close.

"No, honey. We'll make sure he comes home too."

Ann was still reluctant to leave. Both men were watching her, taking their cues from her. After several minutes she smiled bravely at them and taking each by the hand, they walked back to the car. Gunner trailed a few steps behind. Ann looked back once, hoping that very soon all the people she loved would be together.

No one spoke as they drove away, each deep in their own thoughts. Bryce was profoundly grateful to Mark and was more determined than ever to be a friend to him.

Ann felt a sorrow leave her that she hadn't known she still carried. Mark was just...happy and it was a feeling that was new to him.

Chapter 66

The day was beautiful as they headed east toward the harbor. *Now what is Mark up to?* Ann wondered. *He acts like the cat that swallowed the canary.* They parked in the lot of a private marina where there were many boats of all sizes...and prices!

The very last boat wasn't quite as big as some of the others, but its graceful lines appealed to Ann. As they walked closer Ann stopped and gasped. The name neatly printed across the bow was *The Kathy Ann.*

Mark loosened the lines that held the small craft to the dock and hopped aboard.

"You told me when you were nothing but a kid that you had always wanted to ride in a boat and go fishing...so let's go."

Ann and Bryce stood on the dock in a state of amazement as they looked down at Mark who now had a silly lopsided grin across his face. Ann finally leaned forward and Mark took her around the waist, easily swinging her onto the deck of the boat.

Then he offered a hand to Bryce. He didn't want either of them falling overboard before they even left the dock. Gunner took one long leap, landing on the deck. Once everyone was aboard, Mark expertly navigated the boat out to sea.

The sun sparkled on the water and as they picked up speed, the wind lifted Ann's hair and sent it flying around her face. She clung to Bryce, who in turn, held fast to the rail. Neither of them were experienced sailors. Gunner put his nose into the wind and acted like he sailed every day. No big deal.

As they got used to the up and down motion of the boat hitting the waves, they both relaxed and began to enjoy the ride. Mark asked Ann if she wanted to drive the boat and of course she did.

He motioned her to come and stand in front of him. He reached around her and put his hands over hers as he guided her through some careful turns and showed her how to operate the throttle.

She loved going fast and before Mark could stop her, she powered the big engine up and they went skimming over the water. Both men laughed at the excitement on her face.

After a few minutes of break-neck speed, Ann slowed the boat down and Bryce took a turn at the wheel. Finally, Mark signaled a stop and he tossed the anchor over the side. He went below deck and came back with a couple of deep sea fishing poles and some bait.

Ann was game for putting the bait on her hook and did a fairly good job of it. After all she had gutted a deer once, so this was child's play. Since there were only two poles, Bryce stood behind Ann, his arms around her waist. If she did manage to catch something, he didn't want her to go flying over the side.

Mark got the first hit of the day and pulled in a fairly good-sized fish. He took the hook out and threw it back. What were they going to do with it anyway? The fishing was just for fun.

Something tugged at Ann's line and she started reeling. Her fish was small, but it had been exciting to catch it. It must have been the wrong time of day or something because…no more fish. It really didn't matter. They had a wonderful time and that was all that mattered. Ann did, however, take a fair amount of teasing about the size of her bait being bigger than the fish she caught.

They stopped on the way home and ate at a little hot dog place. They were all famished from the salt air and sunshine. At least a half dozen hot dogs were consumed and the frosty root beer was delicious.

Even though Ann had used sunscreen and had also smeared a generous amount on Bryce, they were both rather pink, especially Ann. She looked beautiful and happy to Mark and Bryce. Both were well-satisfied with the events of the day.

They got home a little after dark and after they had cleaned up and Ann had gotten the tangles out of her hair, they gathered in the living room, soon deciding they needed to polish off the rest of the ice cream and syrup.

Ann and Bryce would be flying out in the morning and there was one thing Mark wanted to clarify before he made the final decision to change his life completely by moving to Cedarville.

It would be a sensitive issue to discuss and he didn't know quite how to bring it up. Ann noticed him stirring his ice cream around as he stared intently at the contents of his bowl. She knew something was bothering him.

"Mark", she said gently. "Is everything okay?"

He finally looked at them both and with a sigh he put his bowl on the coffee table.

"I just want to make certain of one thing," he said hesitantly.

He looked away and swallowed before he started to speak. He decided the best approach was just to come out with the truth and let the chips fall where they may.

"I have been in love with you, Ka...Ann since you were seventeen years old."

He paused waiting for a reaction from Bryce. When none came, encouraged, he continued.

"I just want you both to be absolutely sure, knowing how I feel, that you really want me to be a part of your family. Bryce, I want you to know that I have the deepest respect for you and your relationship with Ann. I would never do anything to intrude on that. I would never compromise Ann in any way. What you two have is rare and special. I can't say I don't envy you, but I am content knowing that she is protected and loved by a decent and honorable man."

Having said his piece, Mark sat quietly.

"We want you to come, Mark," Bryce said.

Ann nodded, unable to say anything. A look of relief spread across Mark's face.

"Well, okay then, what time is Thanksgiving dinner?"

***

Mark took them to the airport the next morning and helped Bryce carry the bags inside. For the return trip, they were using the Stratton Industry private jet, a part of Peterson Enterprise, so they could take all the time they needed to board.

Bryce had acquired Stratton Industry upon the death of his father-in-law, infuriating his first wife, Monica. She had expected everything her father had would be willed to her. Not so. Mr. Stratton knew his daughter well. She would have gone through the money and bankrupted the business had he left everything to her. He had trusted Bryce.

The jet was used mostly for business, but today it came in handy for pleasure.

Mark and Bryce shook hands warmly and having exchanged phone numbers, Bryce promised to call and let Mark know what the plan was on their end. Mark in turn would make arrangements for coverage at the hospital.

Mark hugged Ann tight just for a second and then stepped back. He missed her already and she hadn't even left yet! It was only about a month until Thanksgiving and he would have plenty to do to keep his mind occupied...but still...

As soon as the plane was off the ground, Ann laced her fingers through Bryce's and with her head resting against his shoulder, she fell asleep.

The last few days had been emotionally draining for her and she just couldn't manage to stay awake any longer. Bryce put his head back against the seat and closed his eyes. He couldn't be happier.

Gunner was curled up on the seat next to Ann. It was a tight fix but he managed. He rested his head on his paws, yawned, sighed and he too was soon asleep, content that his mistress was safe and sound.

Chapter 67

L uke met them at the airport in Dixon. During the drive home from the airport, Ann, having gotten her second wind, told Luke all about their visit. She talked about Mark, the baby's grave, the boat and best of all, Mark was coming for Thanksgiving.

"I can hardly wait to introduce him to you and the rest of the family," she said excitedly.

Luke, being in charge of security for all of Peterson Enterprise, had been apprised of his mother's past situation, not in great detail, but enough so that if trouble came, he would be prepared.

He was well aware that "Dr. Mark" had saved his mother's life and that, in itself, made Mark okay in his book. If Luke idolized his father, he adored his mother. He couldn't wait to meet the man who had saved her and thank him personally.

They stopped at the ballroom, knowing that on a Sunday afternoon all the family would be there. After hugs and kisses all around and coffee with cookies readily available, Bryce told them that a very good friend was coming for Thanksgiving; a friend of Ann's from "back in the day."

"We are trying to persuade him to move to Cedarville. He doesn't have any family of his own and he's got a serious health issue. He really needs to be surrounded by people who care about him and who will take care of him," Bryce explained. "I know all of you will help Ann and me make him feel welcome and encourage him to stay."

"You don't have to worry about us," Georgio said, speaking for the group. "You know our home is his home. We will be his family."

These people are the most giving people I have ever met, Bruce thought as he looked around the table at each face. *I feel so blessed to be part of it all. I think Granny would be pleased.*

Bryce and Ann had supper with the family before heading up the road to their house. They had only been away for a few days, but it seemed like forever. As soon as the bags were dropped by the door they were quickly in each other's arms for a "welcome home" kiss that lasted...a good, long time.

They were both tired and were soon in bed. Seeing Mark again had brought back memories Ann had worked hard to push to the back of her mind. She couldn't seem to fall asleep. Bryce sensed her pensivenes and getting up on his elbow, he looked down into her face. His hand stroked her hair.

"Are you alright, sweetie?" he asked.

She gave him the smile that made his heart pound.

"Honey, do you know what a remarkable man you are?" Ann whispered.

Bryce dropped his eyes from hers and just shook his head. It was still hard for him to accept a compliment, even from her. Monica had left her mark. Ann held him close tracing the features of his face with her fingertips.

She knew every line, every crinkle around his eyes and the cleft in his chin. She could close her eyes and still see his face. She loved him so much. He had nothing to worry about when it came to Mark. Yes, she had a special place for Mark in her heart, but what she felt for Bryce was so much more. No one could compare to him.

"Sometimes I'm afraid to go to sleep for fear when I wake up this will all have been a wonderful dream," she whispered in his ear.

Over the next hour or so, Bryce gave her reason to believe that what they had was definitely NOT a dream.

Chapter 68

It was the day before Thanksgiving and Mark's plane would be arriving any minute. Ann was so excited she could hardly stand still. They had driven to Dixon to pick him up so they could have a little private time to talk with him before the rest of the family descended on him.

On the ride to Cedarville, he told Ann and Bryce his tentative schedule for closing his medical practice, packing up his things and selling his house in Boston. He had decided he would like his own place in town, so that he could join Ann in her clinic as well as have privileges in the local hospital.

Ann was ecstatic!

"What about the drinking, Mark?" she said quietly. "You can't treat patients in my clinic, or anywhere else, while you're under the influence."

"I know," he replied with a touch of sadness in his voice. "I haven't had a drink today and I have a flight back to Boston on Friday. I won't have another drink. I promise. I'll be stone cold sober by the time I come for Christmas."

"Mark, I suspect you have been drinking for a long time and quitting won't be easy. You could have some serious withdrawal side effects. As a physician, you must know that. I want you to be where I can help you if needed."

"I'll be fine, Ann. Really. You don't have to worry."

But, Ann was worried. She knew, depending on the individual, side effects of withdrawal could occur as soon as two hours after the last drink. Hopefully, he had more time than that. She did a cursory, covert, visual examination of the man sitting beside her.

Nothing too suspicious so far, she thought, *except he keeps rubbing his hands together and licking his lips. Could be a sign of some early anxiety. Wish I could check his pulse, blood pressure and temperature!*

Chapter 69

Anika had been running to the window of the restaurant every time a car went up the road. Finally...

"They're coming! They're coming," she cried as she flew to the door.

The Peterson Clan surrounded the car as soon as it stopped. Mark's eyes popped in surprise.

"Told you," Bryce chuckled. "They have all been waiting to meet you. Hope you're up for it!"

Luke was the first to embrace Mark as soon as he stepped from the car.

"I'm Luke Peterson," he said as he stepped back. "Thank you so much for everything you did for my Mom. I will forever be in your debt. Anything you need, just ask me."

"Come on everyone, let's get inside where it's warm. You will all have your chance to meet our newest family member," Georgio thundered with great enthusiasm.

For the next couple of hours Mark didn't have time to think about how bad he wanted a drink. Everyone was talking excitedly at once until Georgio finally called for order.

Mama poured coffee and put sweet breads and cookies on the table.

"Please, please. Tell us all about yourself," she said.

"Where do I begin?" Mark laughed nervously.

"How about the beginning?" Bobby responded. "We want to know what Mom was like as a little girl."

Ann had told him the family was aware of her difficulties, the trials, the witness protection...all of that. So, without going into the gruesome details, Mark related how he had come to know Ann.

They all sat quietly as they listened to Mark give an abbreviated version of Ann's life from age sixteen as he remembered it. They had all known "Mom" had had a rough childhood and a terrible marriage where abuse was involved, however hearing it from someone who had been there and witnessed it was an entirely different story.

No one spoke for several minutes after Mark finished his story. Each appreciated the man and vowed in their own hearts to help him any way they could.

In typical Anika fashion, the young woman jumped up from her spot at the table. She hugged Mark's neck and kissed him on the cheek.

"Thank you so much for save my Mama," she said.

She had expressed the sentiments of everyone at the table.

"Now I want to hear about all of you; how you all came to know Ann," Mark said, effectively turning the conversation in another, less painful direction.

Each took their turn telling their story. It was obvious they all loved Ann very much. Mark's heart was full of gratitude for this very diverse group. Now he had a good reason for kicking his habit. He wanted to be a part of this family more than he wanted to drink.

Chapter 70

Ann watched Mark closely through the rest of the day. He seemed okay so far, with the exception of getting up frequently to pace. She was afraid he was in for a rough time.

Thanksgiving dinner was served promptly at two the next day. Mark was amazed by all the delicious food. He tried to eat and participate in the conversation at the table, but he was having a difficult time concentrating. His hands had begun to shake and try though he did, he couldn't control it. He began to perspire and his stomach suddenly rebelled.

He excused himself and headed toward the restroom. He made it about ten feet before he collapsed in the throes of a full-blown grand mal seizure.

Ann was immediately by his side. All she could do at this point was to keep him from choking or hurting himself while waiting for the seizure to subside. After the shock abated somewhat, the rest of the family stood ready to follow any instructions Ann gave. Butch and Gunner were on full alert, not knowing exactly what was happening.

"Should we call for an ambulance?" Luke asked calmly.

"No," Ann replied. "I want to stabilize him here and then get him to the clinic. I can treat him there as well as they can in the hospital."

Ann, being board certified in emergency medicine, knew exactly what she was doing medically. But more than that, she wanted to spare Mark the humiliation of a hospital setting, alcohol rehab; the whole gamut of treatment that she knew would be required if he was admitted.

The clinic had been built with two patient rooms that could be used for short patient stays and all the best equipment money could buy was readily available.

She would never jeopardize Mark's safety, however, and if she felt she could not handle the situation she would most definitely make arrangements for him to be hospitalized.

When the seizure finally stopped, the hallucinations began. Bryce had retrieved Ann's medical bag and she immediately administered medication. It took almost an hour to achieve a fragile improvement.

"Okay," Ann said. "Let's get him to the clinic."

Luke had anticipated this request and he had brought the car around to the front door. Luke, Bruce, Bobby and Victor carefully lifted Mark, who was now limp as a rag doll, and got him lying across the back seat of the car. Ann's clinic was across the road and down about a block from the restaurant so the trip was a very short one.

"He will need round-the-clock care for the next several days," Ann explained to the group sitting in the waiting room of the clinic. "He is sedated now and I have intravenous fluids running to keep him hydrated, but he is not out of the woods. In fact, the worst is yet to come."

"We can set up a schedule and take turns staying with him," Georgio suggested.

Everyone agreed to take a turn as long as Ann explained exactly what was required. She would sleep in the other patient room so that she was handy if a crisis arose. Of course, Bryce and Gunner would stay with her.

Georgio and Mama made sure those staying with Mark had plenty of coffee and good food. Of course, the restaurant was still open, dance practice continued, and life went on as normal as possible.

Ann called his office in Boston and told Gladys Mark had become seriously ill and would not be returning home as previously planned.

"Tell Dr. Goodwin not to worry. I will get his patients appointments with one of his colleagues. I hope he feels better soon, and thank you, Mrs. Peterson, for everything."

It took a little over a week before Mark began to make substantial progress.

It had been heartbreaking for Ann to watch him thrashing in the bed calling for Kathy. In his delirium, he saw a young girl, bruised and broken with blood running down her legs, a dead baby on the floor. Even in his hallucinations, he fought to save her.

Only when she sat beside him on the bed, talking quietly about happier times and holding his hand did he relax enough to get some much needed rest. It was not unusual to find Ann dosing in a chair beside his bed.

It was a happy day for everyone when Mark woke up late in the afternoon, his eyes clear, his mind functioning in the real world. He was weak as a kitten, but did manage to sit up in bed with Bryce's help and take some of Mama's hearty chicken broth.

From that time on, he improved almost daily. It was a full out Peterson Clan celebration the first time Mark walked to the dinner table for a meal. He tired quickly, but he was steady, no tremors or sweating. He was on the road to a full recovery.

Mark confessed to Ann that he still craved a drink at times. On those occasions when he felt as if he couldn't control the urge, he sought out one of the family members, usually Ann. Everyone was more than willing to take the time to stay with him until he was back in control.

Chapter 71

While Ann and Bryce were preoccupied with Mark's illness, Luke and Bruce had been busy tracking down Harriet Lewis. They found her in a nursing home not far from her farm outside Boston. She was very ill and completely blind.

The room she occupied, as well as the bed, was filthy. She smelled so bad Luke had to breathe through his mouth to even stay in the room. He was appalled.

Luke laid his hand gently on the old woman's shoulder.

"Mrs. Lewis? Ma'am? I'm Kathy Martin's son, Luke. Do you feel up to talking to me for a couple minutes?"

Harriet roused and opening sightless eyes, she turned her head toward the sound of Luke's voice.

"You're my Kathy's boy?" she mumbled weakly. "Is she all right? I have missed her so much."

"Yes, she's fine. She talks about you a lot and misses you too. Do you feel well enough to answer a couple of questions for me concerning your husband, Maynard?"

"I haven't seen my husband since he left the farm with a promise to come back for me. I have waited all these years..." Her voice trailed off.

A dead end as far as Lewis is concerned, Luke thought as he looked around the shabby room. He shook his head disgustedly. There was no way he was going to leave this woman here in this God-forsaken place one minute longer than necessary. He was well aware of what Harriet meant to his mother.

He asked to speak to the person in charge. Luke became more furious with every passing minute of the half hour Arnold Sherman kept him waiting in a cramped, stifling little office down the hall from Harriet's room.

Sherman offered his hand. Luke ignored it.

"Mr. Sherman, the care of the residents here, or lack thereof, will be duly reported to the appropriate authorities. I will do everything in my power to make sure this establishment is shut down and the residents taken to other places where they will get the necessary care. You should be ashamed."

"Now you see here young man..." Arnold Sherman stammered. "I will have you know we give excellent care..." That's as far as he got.

"I am taking Mrs. Lewis out of here today. Do you understand?" Luke stated through clenched teeth.

"You have no right to do that without the resident's permission," the little weasel of a man whined.

Arnold was a little, rat-faced man with a bad comb-over who tried his best to stand up to Luke and Bruce. No contest.

"Well, let's just see what Harriet wants," Luke countered, his voice getting louder and more forceful as he took a step into the little man's personal space.

Bruce grabbed the little man by his coat collar and marched him down the hall to Harriet's room.

"Take you hands off me this instant," Arnold yelled.

"Shut up. You're in trouble up to your skinny little neck," Bruce barked. "You have bigger problems than me."

Kneeling down on the filthy floor beside Harriet's bed, Luke spoke softly to the frail, old woman.

"Mrs. Lewis?" he asked. "Would you like to go live with Kathy?"

Harriet immediately brightened. She grasped the front of Luke's shirt with surprising strength.

"Oh, yes, please! Take me to Kathy," she managed to say before she sank back down onto the thin mattress.

"Good enough for you, Mr. Sherman? We're out of here."

Arrangements were made for an ambulance to transport Harriet from the Golden Age Nursing Home to the airport where she would be flown to Dixon Airport. From there, another ambulance would be waiting to take her to Ann's clinic in Cedarville. Luke was pretty sure just by looking at her that she needed more care than she had been getting. And where was her money going?

As Luke and Bruce followed the ambulance in their rental car, Bruce contacted the Health Department and reported the nursing home and Arnold Sherman. He was assured the situation would be addressed ASAP and the residents removed to other facilities forthwith. A written report would follow.

When Ann got the call from Luke that Harriet was on her way by ambulance to the clinic, she nearly fainted. Luke did his best to prepare her for, what he knew, would be a terrible shock. He wasn't entirely sure Harriet would even survive the long trip to Cedarville.

Chapter 72

"Honey," Bryce said, as he pulled Ann close. "Maybe it would be easier for us to care for Harriet if we brought her here to the house. We could put a hospital bed in the spare room. I'm sure Victor and Bobby would help us get all the equipment from the clinic that you might need."

Tears filled Ann's eyes.

"Oh Bryce, that's the perfect solution. I really am worn out from the long periods of time without sleep while caring for Mark. I don't regret that for one second, but it did wear me down. It would certainly be easier for me to be able to rest in my own bed. Thank you so much, sweetheart."

Luke was notified of the change in plans.

"Okay, Dad. We are going to take it slow, so you probably have at least ninety minutes before we get there. Harriet is holding on. I think the thought of seeing 'Kathy' again is what's keeping her going."

It took Victor and Bobby about an hour to move a hospital bed, IV poles and supplies, EKG machine, oxygen tanks and everything else on Ann's list. They were ready when the ambulance pulled up the driveway.

Chapter 73

With one look, Ann knew that her friend did not have long. All she would be able to do was give her comfort care. On Ann's orders by phone, the EMT's had done an EKG in the ambulance, put Harriet on two liters of oxygen and started an IV drip. It wouldn't be enough to save her life and she was unconscious upon arrival.

As soon as Harriet was carefully put into bed, Ann drew several tubes of blood, sending them via Bobby to the hospital with a request to process it STAT and call her with the results. In about a half an hour, with the results back, Ann started the appropriate medications. Now all she could do was wait.

After the third day of Ann's tender, loving care, Harriet rallied. She recognized Ann's voice and tears ran down her thin cheeks.

"I thought I would never see you again," Harriet said in a voice so weak Ann had to put her ear to the frail woman's lips in order to catch the words.

"You're going to be just fine. I'll take care of you so you don't have to worry about anything except getting your strength back," Ann said, even though she knew in her heart that all her efforts would be in vain.

Around two the following morning, Harriet roused again.

"Kathy, I love you like my own daughter. I'm so happy to be with you again. I can die a content woman knowing you are loved and happy. Please tell Maynard I forgive him and I loved him to the end."

Ann rested her head gently on Harriet's chest, her tears soaking the old woman's blanket. A thin hand came to rest on Ann's head.

That's the way Bryce found them when he went in to check. Harriet was gone. Ann was weeping softly.

"Honey, you did everything you humanly could for Harriet. She died at peace. No one could ask for more."

Harriet was buried in the Peterson cemetery beside Gloria Hamilton. It brought a smile to Ann's face to think of the two women she loved meeting in the hereafter. They had a lot in common, and all the time in the world to get to know each other.

Chapter 74

It had been a month since Harriet's death. Ann decided the best remedy for her grief was to pull herself up by her bootstraps and throw herself back into...life.

Bryce had been wonderful during this time of introspection and sadness. It amazed her again and again how much he cared for her. His patience was infinite, his love, unconditional.

Dance practice began again in earnest. It was surprising how much stamina she and Bryce had lost during the time they had spent caring for Mark and then for Harriet.

Victor's sympathy only went so far.

"Come on. Do again. Practice step one hundred time make good. Two hundred time make ready to compete again," Victor told his weary students one day after a particularly grueling session.

Ann laughed. It felt good to laugh again.

"Okay, Victor. We get it. Two hundred times it is."

Mark watched the practices with interest. Anika finally dragged him by the hand to the middle of the floor.

"If you can walk, you can dance," she assured him as she began to teach him the basic steps of the waltz.

"You do good," Victor commented as he observed the impromptu lesson. "Little more straight posture, don't let, how you say, bum...

stick out so far. You be good dance soon. Now we just need find partner."

Mark took this as a compliment. The exercise would be good for him and when he was concentrating on learning the steps, he forgot how bad he wanted a good stiff drink.

Chapter 75

Dominic Marco watched his nephew, Tony, pace back and forth in front of his desk. Smoke rose lazily from the ever-present fat cigar clenched between his teeth.

"So, Tony. What you think, huh? How do we snatch this Peterson dame?"

When that sniveling dirt bag, Maynard Lewis, had come to him with the proposition of splitting the ransom money they could demand by kidnapping Ann Peterson, he had been skeptical.

Dominic was nobody's fool. He had done his own investigation into the Peterson family. He knew about the manufacturing company they owned in Dixon, the restaurant/ballroom in Cedarville and the estate Bryce Peterson had built for his very beautiful wife. He was impressed.

It had been well over a month and Dominic was anxious to get moving with this deal. After all, time was money.

"I've got it all figured out," Tony exclaimed. "I only need help from one other person to make this work."

"And who exactly would this 'other person' be?" Uncle Dom replied. "And how much money will it cost me? I ain't bringing in another partner for this job."

"That's the beauty of it! It won't cost you one penny. This kid... nobody would miss him if he, say...disappeared. He's expendable. A nobody. A druggie. All I have to do is promise him a line or two of coke and he'll do anything I tell him to do. I'll take the cost of the coke out of my share of the money," Tony exclaimed, his excitement mounting.

"Number one. What makes you think you're getting a share of the money? And number two, who is this kid anyway? Do I know him? Can he be trusted?"

"Corny Kent, we call him. He's a little tweaker who hangs with a bunch of misfits at the old mill outside Cedarville on Route 47. You know where it is, Uncle Dom. It used to be a saw mill back in the day. After the job, he will come to a...shall we say...a bad end? We can dump the body in the sandpit over in Jackson County. Nobody will ever find him, and frankly, I don't think anybody will even look for him."

"And my name will not be connected to any of this, right?" Dominic said, poking his nephew in the chest for emphasis.

"Right, Uncle Dom. I understand completely. You don't have to worry about a thing."

"Okay, Tony. You run with this. If you succeed, I'll give you ten percent of the take. If you can pull it off without compromising my operation, I'll make you one of my lieutenants. If you screw up, you will sink on your own. I will not help you. Understood?"

"Yes, sir. You can count on me," Tony said as he headed for the door of his uncle's office.

Tony got into his new Mustang convertible. Now all he had to do was find Corny.

It shouldn't be too hard to find him, Tony thought to himself. *I darn well better pull this off or I'll lose this fine automobile.*

Chapter 76

Cornelius J. Kent Jr. was the oldest of four children born to Cornelius Sr. and Delores Kent. They were middle class, hard working parents who just didn't have time to spend with Cornelius. His little brother and twin sisters had come along unexpectedly and in quick succession.

His parents had gotten married right out of high school, which Delores now knew had been a mistake. Cornelius Sr. was home only to eat and sleep, spending every spare minute working overtime so he could provide for his family. Delores was a stay-at-home mom, completely overwhelmed and unprepared to care for her four active children.

Unfortunately, young Cornelius was small for his age and not an attractive child. His ears stuck out from his head at an unnatural angle and his front teeth made him look like a chipmunk. His first day of school set the tone for the rest of his life.

"What kind of name is Cornelius anyway?" the kids asked the little boy cowering against the wall of the boy's bathroom.

"That's a sissy name! Are you a little sissy-girl, Cor-nel-ius?" the older boys taunted as they pushed and shoved him until he was crying.

"I told you he was a cry baby," Randy, the biggest of the older boys yelled. "You are going to be my little bitch. Do you hear me, Cor-nel-ius?"

"Please don't hurt me," Cornelius sobbed "I'll do anything you say, but please don't hurt me."

And he did do everything he was told to do, including "bending over" in the bathroom whenever the bigger boys "wanted some." His shame ran so deep he was unable to look anyone in the eyes.

It didn't help his situation that his younger siblings couldn't pronounce Cornelius, so they called him "Corny."

When Randy heard this he laughed so hard he fell down holding his stomach. Soon the whole school knew and even the teachers took to calling him Corny. The kids made up names for him. They called him Corn-ball, Corn-alicious, Corn-stalk, Corn-dog, or any other variation of his name that came to mind.

He was tormented, humiliated and physically abused every single day at school. He ate as much as he could hold for breakfast at home because he knew his bag lunch would be taken away from him before he could eat it.

Most of the time the sandwich and cookies weren't even eaten by the other kids. They were thrown on the ground and stomped into the dirt. He hated his school mates, his teachers and himself.

He never told his parents what was going on at school, knowing they would only make things worse for him by going to the school board and complaining. The kids would somehow find out and his life would become worse than the hell it already was.

His teachers didn't seem to notice or care. They were too busy helping and praising the "popular kids" to give any time or attention to Corny. He was frequently sent to the principal's office for failing grades even though he wasn't a stupid child; only hopeless and unmotivated. Even the people in the guidance office didn't seem to notice a little boy who was so withdrawn and pathetic appearing.

The girls were as bad as the boys. They would snicker and point at him. He just hung his head and tried to be invisible. Nobody helped. Nobody intervened. Nobody cared.

As he got older, every night was spent fantasizing about what he would do to these kids who incessantly bullied him. He would torture and eventually kill the boys. He would rape the girls, humiliating them just like they did him.

When he was old enough, he dropped out of school and left home. Finding other kids like himself proved easier than you would think. There were a lot of kids out there who felt the same way he did. They didn't seem to fit anywhere else so they banded together and lived in the old mill outside Cedarville.

They survived by shoplifting or ransacking empty houses while the owners were at work or out of town. Often, they did their raiding in other towns that were close by, thus evading the police.

Cornelius never did grow to be very tall. However, he quickly became the leader of his pack of friends by being ruthless and cruel. He carried a knife he had "borrowed" from his father's sock drawer before he left home. He wasn't afraid to use it on anyone who tried to give him any trouble. The power felt amazingly good.

Chapter 77

While Tony was putting together the final pieces of his plan to kidnap Ann Peterson, life had returned to normal for Ann, Bryce and the rest of the family. They were competing again and, as a team, moving slowly up the ladder toward first place.

Georgio and Rosa were the only couple who consistently scored in the top five in any competition; a fact Georgio good-naturedly mentioned frequently to Bobby and Victor.

"So, you youngsters need to watch this old man," he teased. "Maybe you'll learn a little something about hip action and posture."

No one took offense. Not even those to whom the comments were directed.

Victor was late for the morning practice session, something that had never happened before. Ann was beginning to get concerned when he appeared holding a tattered piece of paper. Anika's eyes were red and puffy from crying. *What on earth could be wrong?* Ann wondered as she hurried toward the obviously distraught young couple.

"My Mama, she is too much sick," Victor blurted out with tears running down his face. "I just get letter from friend of Mama, it take long time to get here. She dead maybe by now. I not know what to do!"

"Oh, Victor, I'm so sorry. Let me get some information about your mother and I'll call Oscar and see what he would suggest we do to help her," Ann offered.

After writing down some general information about Helena Petrov's last known whereabouts, her birth date and the correct spelling of her name, Ann got on the phone with Oscar, the family attorney.

After explaining the situation, Oscar was more than willing to do what he could.

"I'll make some calls, look at international regulations...do you know if she has a passport? Probably not. I'll call you back as soon as I have information for you, Ann."

If anyone could help, Ann knew that man was Oscar Schwartz. He, along with Dr. Mark, had saved her life and given her a chance for a future. She had total confidence in this little Jewish attorney and knew everything would work out for the best.

Ann hugged Victor and then Anika.

"Oscar will help us, Victor. Try not to worry, even though I know that's easy to say, but hard to do."

As they went through practice, everyone knew Victor's heart just wasn't in it. Try as he might, he just couldn't pull his mind away for a mental picture of his mother sick, suffering, hungry...even dead.

After practice, Victor and Anika left quietly and headed for their apartment. Victor was going to write a letter to his mother's friend so it would go out in the mail that day.

He wanted more specific information about his mother's condition. It was probably pointless considering how long it had taken her letter to get to him, but he had to do something.

Later that afternoon, Oscar called Ann's private phone.

"I have a friend living in Russia. He owes me a favor and assures me he can find this woman if she is still alive. His men are out looking for her as we speak. Keep your chin up, Peanut. We'll find her. I just hope it's in time to save her."

"Oh, Oscar. Thank you so much. I feel better already," Ann replied.

Bryce didn't have to ask. The look on Ann's face told him that Oscar had the ball rolling and it was only a matter of time before they would know something concrete.

He wrapped his arms around his wife and chuckled.

"I expect we will soon be having a house guest."

Ann snuggled closer.

"I don't think we should say anything to Victor just yet. I don't want to get his hopes up in case the news is bad."

"I think you are probably right, sweetie," Bryce said as he nuzzled her ear. "You are such a wonderful, kind-hearted woman and I'm so proud of you."

Chapter 78

They didn't hear anything until the next evening. Ann and Bryce had just finished supper when the call came.

"Bryce? Oscar here. We found her. It wasn't as difficult as we first thought it would be. She is still living in the same apartment she's lived in for many years, the address Victor gave us. She doesn't look good though. The woman is obviously quite ill. She is refusing to go to the hospital because she doesn't have the money to pay for her care. Plus, she doesn't know or trust my friend. What do you want us to do?"

"Tell her Victor's boss carries health insurance for him and his family, which would certainly include his mother. This was essentially true, although Helena was not technically named on the policy...yet. She doesn't have to worry about the money. Then just take the amount from the general funds budget and pay for whatever she needs. Maybe mentioning her son will prompt her to cooperate. What about a passport?"

"Working on the passport/visa, Bryce. I figured you and Ann would want her to come to the United States so I'm looking for flights and an interpreter to fly with her. I will let you know more about her health issues as soon as I hear anything."

"Okay, Oscar, thanks. We'll wait for your call."

Chapter 79

Where in hell is that little rat-bastard, Corny, anyway? Tony had checked out all the kid's hangouts and nobody had seen him for several days. *He's probably higher than a kite and shacked up with some broad. Damn! I have to get this show on the road before Uncle Dom takes the job away from me,* Tony grumbled to himself.

Corny was, in fact, high on pills and booze. When he surfaced periodically from his drug-induced stupor, he raped the young girl again that he had tied to a bed in an out-of-the-way motel.

He would have to do something with the girl. She just wasn't as much fun anymore. All the fight had gone out of her and Corny liked girls who fought him. It made him feel more powerful when he was able to beat them into submission and then do whatever struck his fancy to them.

The pills were gone and so was his money. He really needed a fix. Soon. He dragged on his dirty jeans, lit a cigarette and sat on the edge of the bed. With his free hand, he pinched the girls nipple until she writhed and whimpered from the pain.

He needed to take a minute to think about his options and he always thought more clearly when he was hurting someone. He smiled at her response, showing a big gap where one of his front teeth was missing.

He decided to just leave the semi-conscious, naked girl in the motel. Someone would find her...or not. He really didn't give a damn one way or another. He was beyond caring if she could identify him. Staying one step ahead of the cops had never been a problem.

Maybe he would get lucky and she would just conveniently die. He had never actually, out-right, killed anybody and he didn't want to start now. After all, he was a user, not a killer. This clever phrase sent him into a fit of laughter over his own creativity.

Upon his arrival back at the mill, one of his minions told him Tony Marco had been around looking for him. A high pitched, manic giggle erupted from his throat. *Tony must have a job for me*, he thought. *What great timing! I need the money!*

Corny called Tony's private number from the pre-paid phone his mentor had provided. Arrangements were made for them to meet on a secluded dirt road off Route 47.

Chapter 80

When Helena Petrov stepped off the plane at the airport, Bryce and Ann had no trouble recognizing her. She was the only one with old clothes, a thin coat and the pallor of illness still evident on her face.

Bryce held up a sign that said "Petrov." The young woman accompanying Helena pointed at the sign and the women started toward them.

The interpreter had to catch the next flight back to Russia and could only stay for the immediate introductions. Ann and Bryce had picked up enough Russian from Victor and Anika to carry on a conversation with Helena as long as it didn't require technical terms of any sort.

"Mrs. Petrov," Bryce said taking her hand in his. "I am Bryce Peterson, Victor's boss and this is my wife, Ann. We would like you to stay with us until you are feeling recovered. Victor doesn't know you are in the United States. We refrained from telling him anything until you arrived safely. He does know you are all right after your treatment in the hospital."

The exhausted woman just nodded her head.

Helena slept soundly for the rest of the day in the guest room of the Peterson Estate. She had arrived with only one small suitcase holding all her earthly belongings. From Victor's description, Ann had bought a nightgown and bathrobe in a size she estimated would fit the tall, thin woman.

Supper that night was pot roast from the crock pot. Helena ate with relish! She savored the strong cup of coffee that Ann poured for her and nibbled on the dessert pastry.

"You are so kind," Helena said with a smile; the first one they had seen.

They could see where Victor got his dark good looks. Helena must have been a very beautiful young woman, because she was a very attractive older woman. Ann was trying to figure out how old she was. *She must be a little younger than Georgio and Rosa,* she decided.

"When can see Victor and Anika?" Helena asked.

Ann explained the tentative plan she and Bryce had put together with the rest of the family...except Victor and Anika. It was going to be a surprise.

A big smile spread across Helena's face. She thought it was a wonderful idea and wanted to know how she could help pull it off.

Ann squeezed the older woman's hand.

"We need to get you an evening gown and shoes, Asia can fix your hair...I'm so excited! Tomorrow, if you're feeling up to it, we'll go into Dixon to my friend Claire's shop. I'm sure she will have something you will like and..."

Helena interrupted.

"No monies to pay. Not get anything unless I pay," the proud woman stated with finality.

I should have thought of that. How would I feel under these circumstances? Ann thought to herself. *How should I word this so that she will feel she is not accepting charity?*

Bryce to the rescue.

"We have a monthly clothing allowance for each couple on the dance team. It's part of their salary. Victor and Anika almost never use all of theirs. They have enough to buy you what you need and I'm very sure that's what they would want. Would that be acceptable?"

"Da," she replied, looking relieved.

Chapter 81

I t was Friday night and the restaurant was filled to capacity as usual. Dinner had been served and the band was warming up for dancing.

Luke stepped to the center of the ballroom floor with his microphone.

"Ladies and gentleman," he began. "Welcome to an evening of dancing at the Vincenzo Restaurant and Ballroom. I'm Luke Peterson."

He smiled and waited until the applause died down.

"Please show your appreciation for our fine musicians directed by our very own, Jimmy O'Brien."

Jimmy accepted the applause and gestured to his band members. The band began to play softly as Luke continued.

"It is my pleasure to introduce you to our very talented dance team. First, we have Victor Petrov and his lovely wife, Anika. They are the leaders and choreographers for our team."

Victor guided Anika into a few dance steps, finishing with a bow from Victor and a deep curtsy from Anika. More applause.

"Next, please welcome Bobby Rodriguez and his lovely wife, Maria."

Bobby, always the comedian, danced a few awkward Cha Cha steps, pretending to stumble. Maria followed a few steps behind with her hands on her hips and shaking her head. This brought a roar of laughter from the audience and enthusiastic applause.

"Our next couple needs no formal introduction. You all know Bryce Peterson and his beautiful wife, Lauren Ann. Better known to me as Mom and Dad."

Everyone rose to their feet with a thunderous ovation as Bryce led Ann onto the dance floor. They bowed several times, graciously accepting the applause, then took their place next to Bobby and Maria.

"Last, but certainly not least, please welcome the founders of Vincenzo's Restaurant and Ballroom, European Ballroom and Latin dance champions, Georgio Vincenzo and his wonderful wife, and 'Mama' to the rest of us, Rosa Vincenzo. With them this evening is our special guest, Russian National Champion in Ballroom and Latin dance...Helena Petrov!"

Georgio proudly walked toward Luke with Mama on one arm and Helena on the other. Both women were dressed in floor length, black gowns. Asia had spent a lot of time on Helena's hair and she looked absolutely stunning. Her eyes were on Victor and Anika.

Victor jerked to attention when he heard his mother's name. It took him a few seconds to trust what was before his eyes. Without regard to the watching guests, he and Anika ran to Helena. Soon all three were hugging, crying and laughing all at once, much to the delight of all those present.

The music swelled and Jimmy invited everyone to come and dance. Luke herded the highly emotional group over to the large round table reserved for the family.

With Victor on one side and Anika on the other, Helena couldn't stop smiling. She was so proud of her tall, handsome son and beautiful daughter-n-law. When Ann looked at Bryce tears were glistening in her eyes. His arm went around her waist and he held her tight.

"I'm so glad everything worked out," he whispered.

He was rewarded with one of her big, beautiful, heart-stopping, eye-popping, dimple dancing smiles.

When Helena was introduced to Dr. Mark, he held her hand just a little longer than necessary. Ann watched with interest. *Well, well, well* she thought. *I will have to encourage this relationship.* The way Helena appraised Mark it was obvious she was impressed. She had been alone a long time and she appreciated a good looking man when she saw one.

Chapter 82

Helena's strength improved almost by the day. It wasn't long before she was helping during practice sessions, giving constructive criticism and encouragement. Her English was quite good, thanks to the travel that was necessary during her days in competitive dancing. She and Mama became fast friends, even though Helena was several years younger.

Helena was soon included in the Family Meetings on Wednesday mornings. It was apparent that she felt confident and accepted by the group, as she frequently made comments and brought forth her ideas.

"When husband and I were young just starting out with competition, coach mention you, Rosa and Georgio many time. You were example of fine technique. We watch you compete when you came to Russia. Never think I meet you in person. You were my...how you say...hero. I often think to self *I want be just like Rosa Vincenzo*."

Rosa blushed. Something she almost never did. Georgio grinned and stroked his mustache.

"Yes, Mama," he said with a faraway look in his eyes. "Those were the days, weren't they?"

"You old fool," she said, trying to sound exasperated.

She touched his cheek fondly as she too remembered those days.

"Mama has offer help with choreography if okay with all of you," Victor interjected. "Maybe we start offer dance lessons, Mama could teach. She very excellent teach."

"It's certainly okay with all of us," Bryce said after looking around the table and getting nods of approval from the rest of the family. "Victor, you work it out and let me know what you need. Just be careful not to take on too much."

It was decided that Helena would have dance class on Tuesday mornings in the ballroom. This new aspect of Vincenzo's would be publicized and potential students could sign up on a first come, first serve basis. They decided to take only four couples to start with and see how it went. Helena could take on more students at her discretion.

If this flies, Bryce thought, *we may have to add some small studios onto the building just for lessons!* He laughed to himself, as he looked over at Ann. *She's loving this! God! What would I ever do without her!*

Chapter 83

The plan was in place and it wasn't complicated. Now if only Corny could remember his part. Tony had gone over it time and time again, making Corny repeat everything. Corny, on the other hand, was only concentrating on his need for a fix. Nothing else mattered right now.

Maybe I should give him just enough to calm him down and then go over it one more time, Tony thought, as he watched the kid pace and rant, repeatedly combing his fingers through his long, greasy hair.

"Okay, Corny. Settle down. I'm going to give you something to make you feel better. After that, you have to pay attention to what I'm telling you. If you don't, I'll get someone who will, and you'll be out the cash. Ya got it?"

"Aaaa, okay, Tony, okay. Ummmm I got it, man. Just give it to me and hurry up. Can't ya see I'm dying here?"

Walking to the car where he kept his stash, Tony snickered. *He'll be dead all right, one way or the other. It's just a matter of timing. And if I time the whole thing just right, he won't have to remember his part. He'll be all strung out and blathering like the idiot he is when I need him to. That's the beauty of my plan. No loose ends.*

I'll have to do some drive-bys so I know when the free clinic is open. Then I'll make my move. Maybe I'll just keep Corny locked up at my place so I'll have him when I need him! Yeah. That's what I'll do. I'll supply him with just enough blow to keep him tied to me.

Chapter 84

A nn and Tess worked together in the free clinic every Tuesday and Thursday morning. As promised, Bryce sat at the front desk. Bobby and Victor couldn't pass up any opportunity to tease Bryce about his new-found skills as a secretary and receptionist.

"So...how's the transcription coming? The filing? That new job of yours must keep you pretty busy," Bobby would say between fits of laughter.

"The pay's not so hot, but the fringe benefits are beyond belief," Bryce would respond glancing at Ann.

Ann joined in the good-natured banter.

"Yes, my love. And you have worked really hard lately. You deserve something extra special."

If the clinic was especially busy, Mark had promised to lend a hand. So far, this had not happened. He had not yet applied for full privileges at the hospital in Cedarville. He had decided he wanted to get back in the game slowly as he recovered from his alcohol addiction.

Tony's surveillance missions had provided him with the information he needed. Every Tuesday and Thursday he drove slowly past the clinic. He wanted to be the last patient of the morning, thus avoiding any other people who might be in the waiting room. His only problem was the dog.

He considered several different scenarios, none of which was satisfactory. *What the hell am I going to do with the damn dog?* He had seen the monster up close and personal. The dog had to be avoided at all costs.

The problem was significant enough that he could ask Uncle Dom what to do, but that made him feel incompetent. Plus, his uncle might think he wasn't up to the task. This was his chance to prove himself. Handling the situation and any complications that arose, was his responsibility.

Chapter 85

Tuesday morning dawned overcast and chilly with rain dripping from the eaves at the Peterson Estate. Ann got up with a sinus headache that abated only slightly with a hot shower and a cup of steaming hot mint tea.

"Honey, why don't you call Tess and make arrangements for Mark to cover this morning? Then you could go back to bed for a while. I'll clean up the kitchen and feed Gunner," Bryce offered sympathetically.

Ann shook her head.

"Thanks for the offer, sweetheart, but I think I'll feel better if I get around and do something useful. Mark hasn't been too forthcoming about helping and if it's busy, I don't want to stick Tess with all the work. I'll be fine. Really."

They got to the clinic promptly at eight o'clock. Tess arrived five minutes after Ann and Bryce. There were already people waiting at the door. It was going to be a busy morning. The security system was deactivated and they were open for business.

Bryce took up his post at the front desk and began taking information from the prospective patients.

Ann put on her white coat, retrieved her stethoscope from her desk drawer and gave the treatment rooms a quick once-over to make sure everything was in its proper place.

"I guess we're ready, Tess. I'll go get our first patient."

Ann gave Gunner a quick pat on the head as she went out to the waiting room. He was in his appointed spot where he could see up and down the hall all the way to the back door.

Chapter 86

I t had been an uneventful morning. Ann and Tess had treated an elderly woman who had a bad cold, a child with an ear infection, a young pregnant woman anxious about her morning nausea... There wasn't anything of a serious nature that had required prolonged attention and the morning passed quickly.

The last patient left the office and Bryce was about to lock the door when he saw a black panel van pulling into the parking lot.

"Looks like we have one more," Bryce called back to Ann and Tess.

Tess sighed deeply. "Okay, one more. Send him back, Bryce."

When the door opened, a tall young man was practically carrying a skinny kid.

"My friend here, is sick. Can he see a doctor right away?" Tony said with a concerned look on his face.

The kid was high. That much was obvious even to Bryce. He was sweating profusely, his eyes were red and glassy and his nose was dripping blood-tinged mucous. Spit was running down his chin and he was talking incoherently. The kid retched once and then proceeded to vomit on the floor.

Ann walked through the door into the waiting room, saw the situation and got a wheelchair. Tony got Corny in the chair, made more difficult by his flailing arms and legs, requiring Tony to hold him down.

Ann headed for the treatment room around the corner from the waiting room and down the hall near the back exit. The closer room had been used for the previous patient and had not yet been cleaned.

Bryce headed in the direction of the utility closet for a bucket, disinfectant and a mop.

"I'll clean up this mess, Ann. Call if you need help,"

Chapter 87

Tony helped Corny onto the treatment table. It had been easier than expected to get in the door. So far, everything was going according to plan.

As Ann leaned over Corny to unbutton his filthy shirt, Tony stepped back and in one fluid movement, his arm went around Ann's shoulders, a knife blade went to her throat.

"Don't make a sound," Tony hissed, "or that bald Don Juan of yours will not live to see another day. Now, very calmly, call the red-headed broad in here."

Ann was immediately terrified. When she hesitated, Tony repeated his command with a low growl through his clenched teeth. For emphasis, he dragged the blade of the knife across Ann's neck just deep enough to draw blood. She knew if she didn't cooperate, he would not hesitate to kill her and then move on to Tess...and Bryce!

She was near panic and she couldn't stop the trembling of her legs or the twisting of her stomach that sent bile up into her throat. She didn't dare scream. If she did, Bryce would come and she had to protect him from this maniac!

Visions of her late husband, Donny Madison, along with his police officer buddies, Art and Willie, moved through her mind unbidden. The wounds from their physical abuse of her had healed, but her mind was another matter entirely. The abuse had been extensive and had gone on for almost three years. She still remembered every minute of it.

Even though she was afraid of what this would mean for Tess, she called in as normal a voice as she could muster considering the circumstances.

"Tess, could you come in here please?"

Those were the last words Ann spoke. She retreated into another world inside her head. A happy place. A safe place. A place where she had always gone when the abuse was too much to bare. She slumped in Tony's arms.

Tess was looking down at a chart she was carrying when she opened the door to the treatment room.

"What's..." She stopped in mid-sentence, a shocked look on her face.

Tony jerked Ann up against his body. *What the f___*, he thought as he got a tighter hold, now needing to support her limp body.

"Don't make a sound or your friend here will die. Understand?"

Tess dropped the chart and raised her hands. All color drained from her face when she saw Ann. Blood had trickled down Ann's neck and had saturated the collar of her pink blouse. It had made its way onto her white lab coat. Tess's first thought was that she was already dead.

"Shut the door," Tony commanded, "and get over here. Sit in that chair."

Corny jumped off the treatment table. Wild eyes flicked over Ann, focusing on the blood on her neck. He licked his dry, cracked lips. His bladder emptied involuntarily; he didn't even notice. The stench in the room rose a notch.

Corny jumped around the room in a frenzy, splashing through the puddle of urine.

"Can I have the gun, Tony? Please? Come on, man, give me the gun. I know what I'm doing. Come on, come on, come on," he whined.

"Shut up you idiot. Find some tape or something and tie that broad to the chair."

Corny immediately began rifling through the drawers of the treatment cart.

"Okay, okay, okay, Tony."

He found a roll of gauze and began wrapping it tightly around and around Tess's wrists. Then he did the same thing to her ankles.

"Okay, Tony. See man? I'm doing it, I'm doing it. Now give me a gun or something. Come on, Tony," he continued to whine, his agitation increasing every minute.

Chapter 88

Tony tossed the knife on the treatment table and pulled a .38 out of his shoulder holster. Corny immediately grabbed the knife and began welding it around like a spear, poking it first at Ann's lifeless appearing face, then Tess's.

If Corny lost control completely, Tony was afraid he would make enough noise to draw the attention of the man who was humming and mopping in the outer room.

"Okay, ladies," Tony said with exaggerated politeness. "This is what we're going to..."

At that moment, while Tony's attention was focused on trying to keep Ann on her feet, Tess threw herself forward in a vain attempt to knock the gun away and loosen Tony's hold on Ann. He turned just in time to hit her on the side of her head with the gun. She crumpled to the floor unconscious, with the chair on top of her. Blood flowed from a gash in her head.

"*Damn!*" Tony swore under his breath. *This is a complication I don't need! And what's wrong with this chick? I hope she didn't go and die on me! Uncle Dom will be furious!*

"Corny, get over here and hold on to this bitch so I can deal with the dog."

Corny wrapped his arms around Ann's chest, groping with one hand, while the other hand held the knife just under her chin. He began grinding his pelvis into her back, moaning in ecstasy, eyes closed.

"Oh, SHIT! Corny, there will be plenty of time for that after we get to the cabin. Come on, Corny. Keep it together!"

Tasers were a wonderful thing. They provided fifty thousand volts of electricity from a distance of fifteen feet, making it the perfect weapon for debilitating the dog.

Tony had spared no expense obtaining the taser with a built-in laser making a miss almost impossible. It would put the dog down, hopefully permanently! He knew he would only get one chance and he had to make it count. Speed was of the essence.

He slowly opened the door a crack. Gunner was standing just a few feet away in the hall. Now was his best chance. Tony stuck his arm out, his finger on the trigger. A red dot appeared on the big dog's chest. Tony fired.

The dog didn't make a sound as he was thrown backwards. The smell of burning dog hair filled Tony's nostrils. Gunner lay on the floor, his body twitching.

Tony threw the door wide open and grabbed Ann, much to Corny's dismay. He would have to carry her to the van.

Corny opened the sliding side door of the van and Tony tossed Ann in like a sack of potatoes, slamming the door behind her. Corny climbed in the passenger seat and they took off out of the parking lot.

Gunner staggered to his feet. Apparently, Tony's aim hadn't been as accurate as required to incapacitate the dog for long. Only one of the probes stuck, delivering only about half the voltage. The other probe hit Gunner's collar where the GPS was located, burning out the circuits. It was now useless for tracking purposes. This didn't mean Gunner came away unscathed. He was hurting.

The back door opened with a push bar and Gunner hit the bar running, causing the door to fly open hitting the outside wall with a bang.

Bryce looked up from his cleanup job, a puzzled frown wrinkling his brow. He looked out the front window in time to see the black van tear out of the driveway and head up the road toward Cedarville.

Just seconds later he saw Gunner running hard after the van.

As realization washed over Bryce, he felt as if someone had punched him in the stomach. He gasped for breath as his mind froze in horror. Somehow he managed to dial Luke's security alert number.

Chapter 89

L uke had just come off duty. He had stopped at the restaurant for a cup of coffee and one of Mama's tasty treats, when he got the frantic call from his father.

Luke immediately initiated a four-way call with Bruce and Biggy, so they could hear what was going on.

"They took Ann. They took her," Bryce screamed into the phone. "I was right here and they took her right out from under my nose. How could I have let that happen? And Tess is injured! Come quick!"

"I'll call for an ambulance, Luke and meet you at the clinic. I'm close by," was Bruce's clipped reply.

"Roger that," Luke responded.

Gravel flew as Bruce pulled his police car out onto the road. Sirens blaring, lights flashing, he headed for the clinic.

"I'll pick up Gunner's GPS signal and see if I can follow him," Biggy yelled into his security phone.

A quick explanation was given to a very startled Georgio as Luke tore out the door. His heart was hammering in his chest as his mind dredged up every horrible image of Tess injured...maybe dying. *And Mom! Who would have the balls to take her?*

Bruce and Luke thundered through the door of the clinic together. Biggy arrived just minutes later.

"In here!" Bryce hollered when he heard the door open.

Luke was not prepared for the amount of blood on the floor around Tess. Bryce was kneeling next to her holding a folded up towel against the gash in her head. He had lifted the chair off her, freed her hands and feet from the gauze and covered her with a blanket.

Minutes later the EMTs rushed into the room.

"Clear the room, please," the lead EMT ordered the four men.

Seeing Tess lying in the pool of blood affected Luke in a way he never expected. She was pale, her eyes were closed and her chest was barely rising with each shallow breath.

At this moment he couldn't even focus his mind on what he had to do. His chest was tight and he felt like he might lose control of all his bodily functions.

Fortunately, Bruce had his wits about him. His Marine training and discipline came to bare and he took charge.

"Bryce, sit down over here and tell me everything that happened. Even the smallest detail could be very important, so please try to concentrate," Bruce said gently. "I know it's hard and I know how upset you are. We'll find her, Bryce. I promise."

He knew he should not have promised he would find Ann, but Bryce was so distraught. He *WOULD* find Ann or die trying.

Luke had gone in the ambulance with Tess. She had regained consciousness on the way to the hospital and had smiled weakly at Luke. His heart melted as relief washed over him. *I'm going to marry this woman,* he thought to himself as he kissed her hand. *Now I have to focus on getting Mom back unharmed or Dad will never recover.*

Biggy had listened intently to everything Bryce said. He had tried to track Gunner, but something was wrong with the GPS that was embedded in his collar. He would have to follow the dog the old fashioned way. With his wits and his instincts. He disappeared without a sound.

Chapter 90

The family had circled the wagons. Bruce took a broken, shaken Bryce back to the restaurant. To say Bryce was distraught was an understatement. Mama hardly recognized him.

He looked like he had aged ten years since the last time she saw him. His skin was ashen and his eyes were so full of despair Mama could hardly look at him. He sobbed unashamedly on her shoulder.

"I can't lose her, Mama. I can't live without her!"

Mama held him tight and patted his back.

"I know, my boy. I know. Try not to worry. Luke and Bruce will find her. We will pray she is not harmed."

Suddenly, wild barking could be heard outside the front door. Anika raced over and threw the door open. Everyone was surprised when Gunner charged in, stopping only long enough to lap up all the water in his bowl.

With water dripping from his chops, he ran to Bruce and began yipping and racing back and forth between Bruce and the door. Being very familiar with the dog's training, Bruce ran after him.

Gunner started an all-out dash up the road, stopping once to look back at Bruce.

I think he knows where Ann was taken, Bruce thought as he jumped in the car and followed Gunner. He had already put out an APB on the van based on the information he had gotten from Bryce.

Every policeman in the county was looking for a black, panel van with the first two letters of the license plate being HF.

It hadn't been all that difficult to identify at least one of the kidnappers based on the description of Corny. The police had interacted with this kid since he was thirteen years old. Everyone knew him. The other guy was a mystery.

Gunner had slowed down to a trot. His tongue was lolling out the side of his mouth.

He's exhausted, Bruce thought. *I hope he can hold on long enough to lead me to Ann...*

Chapter 91

Meanwhile, in a dilapidated cabin hidden in a heavily forested area of the park that abutted the Peterson Estate, Ann had been dragged from the van and tied to a chair. Her chin rested on her chest. Her eyes were vacant.

Hopping around like a fool, Corny was laughing like a hyena.

"We did it, Tony. We freaking did it. We got her. We're going to be rich, man. Now give me some of the good stuff. I need it bad. Come on, Tony. Give it up."

Relieved to have gotten to the cabin without detection, Tony tossed a small bag of high grade cocaine in Corny's direction.

"Make it last you moron. It's all I've got."

Corny grabbed the bag off the floor and hurried to the table in the otherwise empty room. He poured a pile of the white powder onto the filthy table and cut it into two lines. Without hesitation, he snuffed the drug up one nostril and then the other. He slumped to the floor with his back against the wall.

"Aaaahhhhh. That is so good, man. That is sooooo gooooood."

I should have about an hour of peace and quiet before he bounces back, Tony thought. He lit a cigarette. *I have to call Uncle Dom and I can't have a lot of racket in the background.* Walking to the opposite corner of the room away from Corny, Tony flipped opened his cell phone.

"Hey! Uncle Dom. How's it hanging? We got the girl. No problems. How long do you want me to wait before making the ransom call?"

"Let them sweat it out until tomorrow morning. Old man Peterson will be begging to hand over ten million dollars to get his hot, little wife back."

"Are we really going to give her back, Uncle Dom?"

Dominic's laughter was so loud, Tony had to pull the phone back from his ear.

"What do you think?"

He hung up before Tony could come up with an answer.

Chapter 92

The hours dragged for Bryce and the rest of the family. Mama kept the coffee pot filled and a variety of cookies and snacks available. It was all she could think of to do. She had to keep herself busy, otherwise her mind went to Ann and what she was enduring at this moment.

Mama Vincenzo had adopted Ann to her heart. She didn't take the place of her daughter, but she filled that empty spot and Mama loved her dearly. She and Georgio loved Ann and Bryce as if they were their own children.

It broke her heart to watch Bryce as he paced and sobbed. She wished there was something she could do to make it all better...so she made coffee and cookies, but no one had much of an appetite.

It was a Tuesday and the restaurant had to open at six just like any other work day. *Probably a good thing,* Mama thought. *It will give everyone something else to think about.*

The doctor at the Emergency Room told Luke that Tess had a slight concussion and fourteen stitches in her head, but she would be fine. Emotionally, she was a wreck, blaming herself for not being able to help Ann. Nothing Luke said made her feel any better.

It was decided to move the "command center" to the Peterson Estate. The restaurant had to open soon and everyone had their responsibilities. Bruce put a trace on the phones at Vincenzo's as

well as the Peterson Estate. If a call for ransom came in, he wanted
to be able to trace it.

Luke brought Tess to his parent's house so he could watch over
her and his father. He and Bruce had discussed the situation and
come to the conclusion that someone wanted a big payoff from
Bryce.

That was the only scenario that made sense. They had boiled
down the suspect pool to one. Maynard Lewis. How the two
kidnappers were connected to him remained to be seen.

The rest of the family would go about the business of opening the
restaurant for the dinner buffet and dancing. It would be extremely
difficult for them, but it had to be done.

"I know you are all very upset by what has happened, but we
must persevere," Georgio told the rest of the family and the other
staff members. "Ann would be the first person to tell us to carry
on. So...that's what we will do. If there are any new developments,
I will let everyone know. Thank you all for your concern. Mama
and I really appreciate it so much," he finished, wiping the tears that
streamed down his cheeks.

Chapter 93

B ruce followed Gunner to the dirt utility road that ran into the park. He left his squad car along the road and continued to follow on foot. *The tree someone used for surveillance is on this road. There must be something farther back in the woods*, he thought as he crouched low, his legs pumping to keep up with the dog.

Gunner's paws were bloody from running on the macadam. The hair on his chest was singed. He kept going. That's what good K-9 dogs did.

Bruce radioed Biggy. To his surprise, Biggy was close by. All his intel of the surrounding area was paying off. He knew the direction the van had taken and he knew exactly what he would do if he were the kidnappers. Hide in plain sight. The cops would figure he left town. They would never expect him to be so close by. He had to admit, it was a brilliant plan.

"Good boy, Gunner, good boy. Find Ann," Bruce encouraged the dog.

About two miles up the road, Bruce spotted the cabin. The van was parked nearby. *Bingo!*

"Biggy, there's a cabin just up ahead. I'll take the front, you circle round back. Copy that?"

"Copy, Biggy responded. "I'm on the move."

Bruce got close enough to see into the cabin using his binoculars. He could see Ann slumped in a chair. He presumed at the very least, her hands were tied.

Working his way around the structure, he took careful note of where the other windows and doors were. At present, he didn't detect any movement. That could all change in a heartbeat.

Retracing his steps back to the car, he radioed for backup, no sirens or lights. Biggy was instructed to hold his position behind the cabin in case the situation took a turn for the worst. The next call was to Luke.

Bryce answered.

"I found her, Bryce. She looks okay. Put Luke on."

When he hung up the phone, Luke's face was hard. His eyes cold as ice.

"We got the bastard, Dad. I need you to stay here with Tess. I'm going to meet Bruce and the SWAT team."

Before Bryce could protest, Luke was out the door. He knew how bad his father wanted to be there when a rescue attempt was made. However, in his current state of mind, that wasn't an option. He would only be in the way.

There were police cars and the SWAT team van lining the entrance to the dirt road. The guys from SWAT were gearing up. Uniformed officers had erected road blocks and traffic was being rerouted. Two ambulances were waiting...just in case the worst happened. It was obvious that Bruce was calling the shots even with the police chief on the scene.

No one challenged the huge, angry, scar-faced, ex-Marine. Gunner was nearby, alert and watching Bruce, ready to respond to any command.

Luke walked up to Bruce. Neither man smiled.

"What's the plan?"

Chapter 94

Oblivious to what was happening down the road and the fact that every time he walked by the back window, Biggy's sniper rifle was aimed at his head, Tony was feeling very self-important and satisfied.

He had outwitted the police. He would soon be rich beyond his wildest dreams. Contrary to what his uncle thought, he had decided he would take his cut and disappear. He wanted no part of killing the woman. Corny, on the other hand, was a worthless piece of shit. He would be doing the civilized world a favor by offing him.

Corny had "come to" and was a little more under control of himself. His bloodshot, watery eyes turned to Ann. He sauntered over to her and pulled her head up by her hair.

"Hey, bitch. You and me are going to have some fun now. Wake up, damn it. What's the matter with her, Tony?"

"How should I know? Leave her alone. We won't get the money if she's damaged goods."

"The hell with that, man!" Corny yelled.

Ann never moved or said a word as Corny began to lick the blood from her neck. His hands moved roughly over her breasts. He ripped open her blouse.

"Aaahhh. What do we have here? Get a load of these big tits, Tony."

The sucking, slurping noises disgusted Tony. He might be a lot of things, but he wasn't a pervert. All he wanted was the money. That's it. Then let the woman go. Who cares? He would waste Corny. That had been his plan from the beginning anyway.

He glanced over at the silent, disengaged woman. *Maybe I should just do that now,* he thought. *And save myself some aggravation.*

Corny sat straddling Ann's lap, thrusting against her, yelling obscenities at the top of his lungs.

Both men were too engrossed in what they were doing; Corny trying hard to get an erection and Tony watching with a look of loathing on his face, to be aware of the men slowly, quietly surrounding the cabin.

For such a big man, Bruce moved with stealth and cunning, like one of the big cats in the wild stalking its prey. He made it to the front of the cabin, keeping low under the front window next to the door. Very slowly, he lifted his head just enough to peer over the bottom of the window sill.

What he saw enraged him. He had to grit his teeth to keep from putting a bullet in the kid's head. It took several deep breaths before he regained control over his raging anger. There was that little worm, Corny Kent, pumping away while sitting across Ann's lap. He didn't dare take a shot because Ann was in the line of fire.

Gunner had wormed his way, crawling along on his belly, until he was just short of the side window of the shack. Even without direction from Bruce, he seemed to be moving according to his own plan. Tony was within striking distance on the other side of the window.

Biggy and several SWAT team members were covering the back. No way were these scum bags getting away!

Chapter 95

Tony had watched all he could stomach of Corny's perversion. Pulling his .38 out of the holster, he took aim and fired. Blood and brain matter splattered in Ann's face. Corny flew off her lap landing with a thud on the floor, a surprised look on his face. As his vision tunneled down to a pinpoint, he saw the flames of hell waiting for him.

The gunshot was a signal for Gunner to move. He took a running start and went through the window, shards of glass flying everywhere.

When Bruce heard the shot, he kicked the door of the cabin open just in time to see Gunner flying thru the air at a panicked Tony Marco. Tony took a wild shot as he was scrambling backward, away from the dog. Gunner took a hit in the neck. His momentum carried him forward.

Simultaneously, Biggy came crashing through the back window.

Pinned to the floor under the dog's heavy body, Tony screamed for mercy. Bruce looked down at him without sympathy. He rolled Gunner's body off the terrified hoodlum and dragged him to his feet.

The other officers surrounding the shack moved in instantly upon hearing gunfire. Tony had the good sense to know when he had been beaten. He didn't put up any fight.

Bruce took Tony into custody, read him his rights and marched him toward a squad car. Then he went back inside to attend to the dog. His heart was heavy.

He knelt beside Gunner. Tears welled up in his eyes as he laid his hand on the dog's head. Gunner whined and tried to stand.

"You done real good, boy. Ann is safe. You just rest easy now, big fella. I'll take good care of you."

He grabbed a large gauze pad from the EMT and fastened it to the wound in Gunner's neck to stop the bleeding. Bruce carefully picked him up and carried him to a nearby police car.

When the dog was on his way to the vet, Bruce went back to processing evidence. He needed to do something to keep his mind off the dog. Would he live? It was a serious wound.

Bruce had never prayed for an animal. He felt a little silly doing it now. If it would help, he wasn't too proud to try. Maybe this time, God would listen to him.

The situation seemed to be under control. Biggy wanted no part of the follow-up stuff. He was more of an action kind of guy. He disappeared quietly into the forest. He would catch up with Luke and Bruce later to compare notes. It would be a good opportunity to look for holes in their security.

Paramedics were attending to Ann. She was battered and bruised. Her clothes were torn, she had a huge goose-egg on the side of her head, her eyes were glazed over. She did not respond to the EMT's efforts to talk to her.

A police car was dispatched to bring Bryce to the cabin.

When Bryce saw the police car coming up the driveway, he feared the worst. As he went to answer the door, he felt as if his feet were mired in wet cement, his heart about to explode.

"Mr. Peterson?" the officer asked.

All Bryce could manage was a shake of his head to the affirmative.

"Your son asked me to escort you to the crime scene. He's with your wife. She has been rescued and appears to be free of serious injuries. The problem is, she isn't responding to anyone, not even Luke. He's pretty upset as you can well imagine."

If not for the quick reflexes of the young officer, Bryce would have fallen. He could barely stand under the onslaught of emotions running through him.

Chapter 96

S eeing his father in the approaching police car, Luke ran to help him.

"Mom's okay. She really needs you though. She won't talk to anyone and the EMTs need her to answer some questions before they can transport. Dad, she won't even talk to me! I don't think she recognizes anyone!"

Bryce didn't need any more encouragement. Strength returned to his legs as he ran toward the gurney. She looked so small under the blankets they had put over her.

"Ann!" Bryce cried out.

She slowly turned her head until she could see him. She held out her arms. Bryce flew into them. The dam finally broke. She sobbed as she clung to Bryce. His tears mingled with hers as he held her close and stroked her hair.

"Bryce! I knew you would come for me!"

The doctor wanted Ann to stay overnight in the hospital for observation. The CT scan didn't show any problems from hitting her head on the floor of the van when Tony had thrown her in during the kidnapping. The doctor was more afraid for her mental state due to what she had been through than any physical injuries.

Bryce would not leave her side no matter what the doctor said. If he had to sleep on the floor beside her bed, so be it. He would not let her out of his sight...ever again. When Mark arrived, relief swept through them both.

Mark had a discussion with the treating physician.

"I really think Ann would be more comfortable at home. She will never be left alone, I can assure you of that. I'll check in periodically to make sure she's all right."

Valium was prescribed for possible anxiety. Prescription in hand, Ann and Bryce left the hospital. Mark drove them home and stayed until Ann finally fell asleep, curled up on Bryce's lap.

When word had come that Ann had been kidnapped, Mark almost went "off the wagon." He was beside himself with worry. He blamed himself. He had putzed along, comfortable with his life of leisure; no responsibilities. After all, he was in recovery. It was safe not to have to face any of the pressure involved in a medical practice. He deserved a little respite. At least that's what he had told himself.

By the time he arrived back at his apartment, he had given himself a good tongue lashing. *I should have been there. I could have stopped it. No more wiling away the days romancing Helena. From now on, I'll go to the clinic every day it's open!*

Mark wasn't the only one awash with guilt. What Bryce felt was far beyond guilt. He had promised Ann he wouldn't let anything bad happen to her ever again. Every time he looked at her, the burden of that broken promise crushed him anew. Silent tears coursed down his face as he watched her sleep. How was he supposed to live with that?

Chapter 97

The days passed. Ann and Tess healed and life fell back into its familiar rhythms. Everyone seemed to be healing from the ordeal, except for Bryce. He looked more haggard with every passing day. Ann was becoming more and more concerned. The rest of the family was worried by what they saw, but felt powerless to help.

The day Gunner was brought home, limping and with a bandage still around his neck was a bright spot for everyone. He was a hero. After being fussed over for several minutes, he took up his post beside Ann and Bryce. Once a guard dog—always a guard dog. He took his job seriously.

Bryce went about his daily work, the sadness hanging around him like a shroud. He never laughed. He rarely smiled. And if he was protective of Ann before, they were now like Siamese twins.

He even stood outside the bathroom door when she needed the powder room. His state of mind was affecting everyone. Even Georgio wasn't his normal boisterous, happy self.

Things came to a head one night about a month after the kidnapping. Ann was working in the kitchen, cleaning up and putting the left-overs from dinner in the fridge. Bryce usually helped her with these tasks.

She went to their bedroom. There was Bryce sitting on the side of the bed, bent over with his face in his hands, shoulders heaving in an effort to control his fragile emotions.

Sitting down beside him, Ann put her arms around him. She rested her head on his shoulder.

"Bryce, honey, what's wrong?"

"I promised to protect you! I failed miserably. What if you had been killed? How can you ever trust me again?" he choked through his tears.

Ann quickly realized this was her chance to help Bryce and save their life together.

"Oh, my love. You're my hero. It was you who acted quickly to alert Bruce and Luke. It was you who gave an accurate description of the men and their van, even giving a partial license plate number. You rendered first aid to Tess, quite possibly saving her life. You could never have known the intentions of those men. It's not your fault, Bryce."

His head came up. The small flicker of hope in his eyes touched Ann's heart deeply.

"You did everything humanly possible. And you came for me just like I knew you would. I trust you completely. And I love you so much. It kills me to see you blaming yourself. We're both safe and we're together. That's what's important," she reassured him.

His response told Ann everything she needed to know. It looked as though they were going to bed early tonight. They hung out the "do not disturb sign," so to speak, and no one saw them for a couple of days.

Chapter 98

Now that everyone was back to functioning normally, Luke decided it was time to discuss the events surrounding the kidnapping. He wanted everyone's input.

As Biggy had mentioned to him earlier, it was time to find out where the current security had broken down. Georgio suggested they all get together for Sunday dinner, with this discussion to follow.

"I don't want to take time away from our Wednesday meeting, because that's when we talk about business issues," he told Luke. "It will, no doubt, bring back painful memories and I want people to be able to go home knowing they won't have to revisit the subject again."

"That's not completely accurate, Georgio. We will all have to testify at Tony Marco's trial. It won't be easy. What do you think about inviting Oscar to come too? He will be able to give us some guidance with regard to testifying in court."

Georgio clapped Luke on the back.

"Good idea. I'll call him."

The entire family gathered a week later. It was almost like Thanksgiving; Mama had really outdone herself. They all knew what was coming later, but this did not stop them from enjoying all the great food.

All the women brought one of their specialty dishes to supplement Mama's already overflowing menu. Carla brought one of her soul food concoctions; a favorite of Bobby and Maria's. They, in turn, provided a big pot of black beans and rice. Helena brought a Russian dish nobody had ever eaten before. A huge bowl of green salad was Victor and Anika's contribution to the meal. Asia had fixed sweet and sour chicken. Tess brought some kind of healthy vegetable dish, which Luke picked at really carefully to make sure he could identify everything before he ate it.

When Oscar and Mildred arrived, they handed over a couple of bottles of very expensive wine. Ann had prepared one of her famous desserts, which was to be kept a secret until it was time to eat it. Mark, Bruce, and Luke, being bachelors, just brought their appetites.

When everyone was seated and ready to eat, Biggy slid into his place next to Bruce. No one had seen him come in. He had this uncanny ability to appear and disappear without warning. He was still wearing his camo outfit right down to the black grease under his eyes. Guns were not allowed at Mama's table, no matter how much he protested.

"Gosh, Big," Bobby teased. "You didn't have to dress up just for us."

"I'm always on the job, Bobby, always on the job. Ready at any time. You know me," he answered seriously.

Everyone laughed.

"Yeah, we know." Bobby chortled. "Do you ever lighten up?"

"No."

It wasn't the first time he had come to a meeting "dressed for work," as he called it.

Biggy was well-liked by everyone. His idiosyncrasies were accepted. He was a valued member of the team in which they all played an important part.

Chapter 99

Georgio began the meeting after everyone had eaten. Dessert would be saved for later with coffee.

"Luke, why don't you fill us in on where the investigation is headed? Have they found out who was the mastermind behind the whole thing?"

"Tony Marco keeps insisting he ran the show. So far, he refuses to name anyone else besides Corny Kent. He will at least go down for kidnapping and murder. We sure would like to know if anyone else was involved though. Somehow I don't think he came up with this all on his own."

"He has an uncle, Dominic Marco, who is a wanna-be mobster," Bruce interjected. "We are in the process of checking him out. So far, we haven't found anything to implicate him in the kidnapping. He's sleazy, but smart. When we brought him in for questioning, he said he didn't know anything about the plan to kidnap Ann and we couldn't prove otherwise."

"We couldn't hold him without evidence of the crime," Luke continued. "We are looking for Maynard Lewis though. He was high on our suspect list as a person who would want revenge against Mom even before the actual kidnapping. We'll turn over every rock until we find him!"

Biggy fired off the next question.

"So where did our security fail? Anyone have suggestions?"

"I don't think the security we had in place failed necessarily," Georgio said.

"Gunner certainly did his job. Bryce responded quickly and provided excellent information about the kidnappers and their transportation. Luke, Bruce and the rest of the police officers were Johnny-on-the-spot. And you did everything you could, Biggy. I'm not sure what else we could have done."

Mark spoke up for the first time.

"I take some of the responsibility for what happened. I should have been there. It has always been considered part of my recovery that I would spend time working at the clinic. I haven't been very good about following through with that. From now on, I will be there whenever the clinic is open. And, Ann. I am so very sorry."

"Thanks, Mark," Bryce said. "But there is enough guilt to go around. I was right there after all and didn't even know what was happening!"

Georgio shook his head sadly.

"Well, hindsight is always 20-20, as they say. Let's just be thankful everything turned out okay and Ann is safely back with us. Blaming ourselves isn't going to solve anything. Now we need to focus on coming up with ideas to prevent it from ever happening again."

"I have already put in the paperwork for another guard dog. I should have a response soon. Gunner proved invaluable, but I'm not sure how effective he can be now that he has been injured. He may very well have some permanent limitations. Paying for another dog will have to come out of the Peterson Enterprise budget, and it won't be cheap," Luke finished.

"I don't think money will be an issue," Bryce answered. "Just let John know how much you need."

Oscar posed a good question. "What about the motion sensitive cameras at each exit? Were they functioning properly? And what about Gunner's collar? I thought it was supposed to be able to transmit a signal that could be tracked."

Bryce ran his hand down his face. This was very hard for him. Even though everyone had assured him that he was not at fault for what happened, he still felt the burden of responsibility for letting the situation get away from him.

"Yes, the cameras were functioning properly. However unless you're looking at the monitor all the time... With other work to be done and patients coming and going, watching the monitor every minute just isn't feasible. I'm not trying to make excuses. I should have been paying more attention. I glance at the monitor occasionally..." His voice trailed off.

Ann's heart ached for this man she loved so much. She knew exactly how he felt. She would feel the same way if the situation was reversed. She squeezed his hand.

"When Marco fired off the taser, one of the probes hit the transmitter on Gunner's collar. The result was a burned out GPS. It's a good thing too. If Gunner had been hit with the full fifty thousand volts, he probably wouldn't have made it," Bruce explained. "There isn't anything we could have done about it. Fortunately, Gunner is one smart dog!"

Tess had been sitting quietly beside Luke listening to all the comments and suggestions.

"I think we should have some kind of 'panic button' in every treatment room located out of sight, but easily accessible. That way if we have trouble we can immediately signal for help. The person at the front desk will know immediately something is wrong without having to depend on watching the monitor constantly."

"Great idea, Tess. What do you think, Luke? Can we put that into effect right away?" Bryce said.

Luke looked at her with pride. "That IS a good idea, Tess. By the time we ran the tapes from the cameras, Dad had already told us everything we needed to know. I think we should make the panic buttons our first priority. In fact, it might be a good idea to install them in other areas of Peterson Enterprise. The alert could be transmitted to the security devices we all carry. We could also program the cameras to emit a signal of some kind when movement is detected. What do you think, Bobby?"

"Yes, that's another good suggestion," was Bobby's enthusiastic reply. "I'll get right on it."

This is like closing the barn door after the horse is gone, Mama thought to herself. She sighed. She would never say that out loud. The whole thing had been devastating enough, especially for Bryce. For once, she would keep her comments to herself,

"What about gun?" Helena stated quietly. "One in each room."

Everyone was silent for several seconds. Some were not sure they wanted to go quite that far. Finally Biggy spoke up.

"I can make that happen. No problem. I'll give all of you lessons on safe gun handling and train you on the use of a gun for personal protection."

No one else had any other suggestions to offer so it was unanimously decided to put all the measures into effect ASAP.

"Now let's have dessert," Bobby shouted.

That comment broke the tension in the room and everyone relaxed. Mama just shook her head.

"You people," she muttered, a smile in her eyes as she tried to look disgusted.

She and Ann headed for the kitchen to dish up Ann's pineapple-upside-down cake. As was now his usual, Bryce followed his wife. Gunner limped along not far behind.

Chapter 100

Tony's one call had been made to his uncle Dominic.

"I told you, Tony, if you screwed up you were on your own. Well...you're on your own. I'll give you the name of a good defense lawyer and that's it. You keep your mouth shut! If you implicate me in any way, you're a dead man and I don't care if you are my nephew! Maynard Lewis will have a tragic accident, but that is only to protect ME. Lewis will sing like a canary if he's questioned and I'm not about to let that happen."

With that said, Dominic Marco hung up. His next order was for one of this thugs to "take care of" Maynard Lewis.

Two weeks later, the police and fire department responded to a fire in a rundown motel outside town where Lewis had moved when the kidnapping plan was in place. He wanted to be near "his money." One body was found in the ashes. It was later identified as Maynard Lewis. On autopsy, a bullet hole was discovered in the back of his head.

On his lawyer's recommendation, Tony Marco plead guilty to charges of kidnapping and murder in exchange for a life sentence as opposed to the death penalty. What choice did he have? There were lots of eye witnesses. A jury was sure to convict him.

He would take the fall all by himself. All his dreams of grandeur ended as he put on the orange jumpsuit marking him as a prisoner at the Vermont Northern State Correctional Facility.

Due to bad behavior, which included stabbing another inmate, inciting a riot in the exercise yard and passing along contraband, he was later transferred to the ultra-maximum-security, or "supermax" facility, Southport Correctional Facility in Upstate New York.

It was not unusual for the Vermont Department of Corrections to send inmates out of state to larger facilities where housing them was more cost effective. Besides, Tony had proven to be an uncooperative inmate and they were glad to be rid of him. He would spend the rest of his life behind bars.

His guilty plea ended it for the Peterson family. No one would have to testify, which was a huge relief, especially for Ann. She had been down that road before. She wasn't positive she could do it again.

Chapter 101

All the new security measures had been installed, much to Ann's relief. As promised, Mark was at the clinic every day they were open. He had returned to good health as the effects of his alcoholism subsided.

He was still a very handsome man and Ann had noticed how much time he was spending with Helena. He had even signed up for dance lessons. The fact that Helena had moved his name to the top of the list of prospective students wasn't lost on anyone.

Dance competition was in full swing again after a brief hiatus during the all-consuming events surrounding the kidnapping. The story had run in all the newspapers around the country, only adding to the mystique of the "King and Queen of Romance." The Petersons took it in stride, trying to focus on the dancing and not so much on the publicity they were getting.

Bobby, on the other hand, was ecstatic.

"Yo, man. Free publicity. We went through a lot to get it, we should capitalize on it, don't ya think?

Georgio laughed so hard he had to wipe his eyes.

"Bobby, my boy. We can always count on you to put a positive spin on any situation!"

Regardless of what anyone thought about it, reservations flooded in. Even the waiting list took up several pages.

When Ann and Bryce competed, the venue was packed to the doors. Everyone wanted to get a look at the popular couple and possibly get an autograph. It got to the point where they needed a security detail just to disembark from their limo!

Everyone on the team had started to place in the top five couples, not due to their notoriety, but because they had been working hard. Practice sessions were often long and exhausting. Helena proved to be a harder task-master than her son. She wanted perfection from her team and she was going to get it...or else.

Except when he was working, Luke and Tess were inseparable. *Love is in the air,* Ann thought. *I'm so pleased for Mark and Helena. They both deserve to be happy. And I couldn't have picked a better match for Luke*

Chapter 102

B
ruce and Luke went to the Dixon Airport to pick up the new dog that had been shipped from Germany. They had been notified when the dog was in route and the arrival date and time. They had not been told any other details.

She was a beautiful German Shepherd, almost matching Gunner in size. Both men were impressed. They were anxious to put her through her paces. Her name was Angel. She was handed off to Bruce by her German trainer, along with the "instruction manual," as Bruce called it.

They worked with her alone for a couple of weeks to get her acquainted with her new handlers. Then they brought her to meet the rest of the family at a Wednesday family meeting.

The minute she entered, Gunner and Butch stood at attention, sniffing the air and using all their powers of persuasion to gain favor with the newcomer. All the laughter that followed did not distract the two male dogs from "admiring" the new female addition to the team. Bruce and Luke made sure all concerned behaved properly.

I should probably get Gunner and Butch neutered, Bruce thought to himself. *I sure hate to do that though. Maybe after a litter of pups. We could breed them, train them and sell them to other private organizations looking for security dogs. I'll have to discuss the idea with the rest of the family. We may even need to hire some additional staff.*

After the initial excitement over the dogs died down, Luke stood up. He had everyone's attention.

"After what happened several weeks ago, I've been doing a lot of thinking about what's important. I've come to the conclusion that relationships should be at the top of the list. If we don't have each other...well, life wouldn't be worth much."

He reached down and lifted Tess to her feet. As she stood beside him, he dropped to one knee. He pulled a small box from his pocket and flipped it open.

"Tess, would you do me the honor of becoming my wife? I have realized over the past weeks, how utterly bleak my life would be without you."

The ring was large, but not too large. It sparkled in the light. Tess looked from the ring to Luke's face and back to the ring. She covered her face with her hands and began to cry softly. After several uncomfortable seconds went by, especially for Luke, she gave her answer.

"Luke, I have loved you from the day you picked me up at the hospital when Victor and Anika first arrived. What on earth took you so long to see the light? Of course I'll marry you."

Luke was immediately on his feet and sweeping Tess into his arms. He kissed her with vigor to the cat-calls, laughing, hollering and general chaos from the rest of the family, Bobby being the ringleader.

Tears glistened in Ann's eyes as she remembered the day Bryce had asked her this same question. When their eyes met, she knew he was remembering too. He used this happy announcement as an excuse to kiss his beautiful wife. Victor, Bobby, John and Georgio followed suit, much to the delight of the ladies present.

After order was restored, everyone was surprised when Bruce slowly got to his feet. He hemmed and hawed for several seconds before pulling Asia to her feet beside him.

"Well...ah. I ah... That is Asia and I," he stammered. "We went to the courthouse yesterday and ah...we got married," he finished as a huge grin spread across his face.

Asia looked like a little porcelain doll standing next to the huge, mountain of a man. Two people couldn't look more different. How they felt about each other was obvious and transcended their differences.

Pandemonium broke loose once again. Everyone was talking at once. Congratulations went out to both couples.

Mama clasped her hands to her chest as if she were having some kind of attack.

"Praise be!" she said. "Papa, just look at our kids. They make me so happy!"

Apparently, there was one more surprise. Mark stood up and looked around at all the puzzled faces.

"Helena and I..." he began. "It seems all of you beat me to the punch."

Helena was smiling up at him. All of a sudden everyone made the connection at the same time, but no one said a word. Anika was the first to recover her voice.

She ran around the table and threw her arms around Mark's neck.

"Oh, this wonderful! I so happy."

Then she hugged Helena. Soon all the ladies were crying and hugging one another. The men were looking well-satisfied with the fervor they had created. It couldn't have gone any better if they had planned it this way.

"What about you, Biggy? Do you have a woman waiting in the wings that we don't know about?" Bobby hollered across the table.

"Are you kidding? Hell, no. I tried it four times and there isn't a woman alive who will put up with me," he quickly replied, looking totally put upon. "The whole marriage thing scares me to death. I don't mind admitting it. Already done it, didn't like it, won't ever do it again!"

Laughter erupted again. Biggy quietly slipped away, grumbling to himself. He wanted no part of all this hoopla.

Georgio sat back and watched all the excitement with a merry twinkle in his eyes.

"Ah, Mama. Who would have thought! We best get ready for babies!"

Rosa slapped his arm.

"You old fool. Let them get married first before you go planning future grandchildren."

Her attempts at seriousness failed utterly. She was beyond thrilled. She never thought she would recover after her Little Rose died, but God had a way of working things out. She made the sign of the cross and said a little prayer of thanksgiving as she looked around at her ever-expanding family.

"Dear, Lord," she prayed. "I am so grateful for the wonderful family you have given me. This is all that matters!"

The Sweet Ever After Series presents
the third and final book,

For All Time

Luke Peterson and Theresa O'Shay tie the knot.

Gunner becomes a proud papa.

Luke and Bruce open Peterson Search and Rescue.

Ann and Bryce become grandparents to a special needs child.

Two abused and abandoned children find a home.

And the end of Vincenzo's Restaurant and Ballroom as we know it.